THE
Dark Garden
MARGARET BUFFIE

KIDS CAN PRESS

For Jim

First U.S. edition 1997

The author acknowledges the support of the Canada Council during the writing of *The Dark Garden*.

Kids Can Press acknowledges the financial support of the Ontario Arts Council, the Canada Council for the Arts and the Government of Canada, through the BPIDP, for our publishing activity.

Published in Canada by
Kids Can Press Ltd.
29 Birch Avenue
Toronto, ON M4V 1E2

Published in the U.S. by
Kids Can Press Ltd.
2250 Military Road
Tonawanda, NY 14150

www.kidscanpress.com

Edited by Charis Wahl
Interior designed by Tom Dart/First Folio Resource Group, Inc.
Printed and bound in Canada

CM 95 0 9 8 7 6 5 4 3 2
CM PA 01 0 9 8 7 6 5 4 3 2 1

National Library of Canada Cataloguing in Publication Data

Buffie, Margaret
  The dark garden

ISBN 1-55337-091-0

I. Title.

PS8553.U453D3 2001   jC813'.54   C2001-930176-6
PZ7.B83Da 2001

Kids Can Press is a Nelvana company

Willows whiten, aspens quiver,
Little breezes dusk and shiver
Thro' the wave that runs for ever
By the island in the river
        Flowing down to Camelot.
Four gray walls, and four gray towers,
Overlook a space of flowers,
And the silent isle imbowers
        The Lady of Shalott.

The Lady of Shalott
Alfred, Lord Tennyson, 1809–1892

PROLOGUE

Sometimes I get little echoes of the time right after the accident — fear? anxiety? surprise? The images come back in flashes — long brown arms in short white sleeves reach out and lift me onto a low cloud that rolls quickly under flickering trees; a siren screams nearby; someone cries, "What's happening? Why don't I know what's happening?"

Something sharp pricks my arm. Silence pounds in my ears. My body lifts into the air. And then I die.

Chapter One

I am in a beautiful night-shadowed garden. I push my toes against the soft earth and rise above the deep green and blue shapes below, and I am in perfect bliss.

Then the shadows slide away from the secret places along the edges of the garden. They close in and talk to me in urgent voices, nudging, coaxing me to leave. I float higher and higher until I surface into a world that is eye-searingly bright and full of medicinal smells and sounds with sharp edges.

When one of the shadows asks me my name nothing comes — just a crackling emptiness. The shadows change into people in pastel clothing who come and go and talk to me and are surprised when I answer them. But not as surprised as I am when the words that slide into my head turn out to be the right ones. They begin their tests. I show them that I can tell a lamp from a tree and a cup from a glass, but over the next few days and nights the white mist that is my memory never changes. At night they leave me alone, and I sink into the garden's green darkness with sweet relief.

In the daylight they come back and ask again and again — do I remember Thea? Her parents? They tell me that Thea is her ... *my* name — Thea Austen Chalmers-Goodall. With a hyphen. I don't know her. I am certain I could never have *been* Thea Austen Chalmers-Goodall. With or without a hyphen.

I am no one.

CHAPTER TWO

It's been three weeks. Everyone is trying to get my memory to kick in — their words, not mine. They have shown me a school yearbook. The narrow face with the high-domed forehead I see in the mirror does look a little like the rounder unsmiling features in the photo they pointed out to me, but how can I be sure it's really me?

They *tell* me I am Thea. Over and over.

Two people come fairly often to visit. They claim to be Thea's — that is, *my* — parents. The woman, Agatha Chalmers, looks too old to be pregnant. Her black hair is mixed with long gray strands, and her neck sags with soft wrinkles — but her belly looks like she's carrying a bedpan under the grubby shirts and baggy stretch pants she wears. She told me on the last visit that there are two kids at home, younger than me.

She seems genuinely happy to see me — for the first five minutes of each visit. She gives me a kiss on the cheek, and after she's asked how I am and I shrug, she tries to get me to talk. Soon she gets restless and starts to pick at things — her nails, her buttons, bits of her clothing.

During these few minutes, she describes how she spends each day. "Simply run ragged," she says. "Absolutely run off my feet." Then, as if she's suddenly remembered something, she announces she must be going. And she's gone.

Today I looked at her closely – at the swollen face and pale freckled hands. Nothing was the least familiar. She is the color orange – busy, unsettled, jumpy.

The man's name is Wilton Goodall. He has limp greyish hair, and his eyes, behind thick round lenses, are vague, as if he can't make up his mind what to say – especially to me.

When they visit together on Sundays, he stands to one side speaking only now and again, usually about things like the weather. He smiles a lot – that is, the ends of his lips turn up – but his eyes stay vague, distracted. He smiles at everyone. He is the color gray – dull, soft, muffled.

Agatha clicks her tongue a lot when he speaks and sometimes she rolls her eyes. Once she told him to be quiet, for heaven's sake, when all he was doing was telling me it was sunny and warm out, and did I remember when he used to take me for what-do-you-call-it ... ice-cream at the corner shop. He didn't say anything back to her, just smiled and gazed out the window at the parking lot.

When he comes alone he's a little more alive. He usually talks about his job – teaching something called theoretical mathematics – going on about how he's been applying some of his ideas at "home," with me. A few days ago he brought in a blue folder with pages of a computer print-out covered in columns and numbers and words.

"We were – that is, you and I were, uh, engaged in working on a new concept of a, well, of a multi-purpose and, uh, functional form of household accounting together, Thea, and I rather *hoped* that, well, perhaps it might activate a memory or two."

I had no idea what he was talking about, but he wouldn't give up, explaining over and over in a gentle drone about how I used to do most of the household finances and how I would do them again after I got home. When he said it was part of his and Agatha's "uh, family policy" to have everyone working together, "pulling their weight," I felt something click in my head. I grabbed the folder and threw it on the floor, where it broke apart and sprayed paper everywhere.

I was as surprised as he was. He kept apologizing as he gathered up the loose papers. I was shaking with anger but didn't know why. So I told him I was tired, turned over and pretended to go to sleep. After he left I lay wide awake.

I don't know these people. I don't remember any folders or columns of numbers. I don't remember him. Or her. Yet they're so weird, how could anyone forget them?

What is going to happen to me?

Dr. Browning, the resident shrink, keeps saying I shouldn't expect miracles overnight. Huh. Miracles. I'd settle for one clear memory.

Tomorrow I have to leave. I have to live at Wilton and Agatha's place. I'll meet their other two kids, Thea's – *my* – two sisters. Will they be as strange as their parents? Am I?

"Going home will be good for you, Thea," Dr. Browning said this morning, beaming. "It should help your memory come back even faster."

"Even faster?" I asked. "You mean faster than dead stop?"

He wasn't amused. Dr. Browning is the color ... yes ... brown. His name suits him. Plain, dull, boring, safe.

So I'm going tomorrow – to Thea's. And I'm scared stiff. I don't want to live with the Gray Accountant and Orange Simply-Run-Ragged Agatha.

Lately the garden has been fading. That scares me more than anything. And last night, instead of the garden, I dreamed of a closed door and a small white fist banging on it – my fist. Someone had locked me in a silent room and taken away the key.

CHAPTER THREE

Wilton Goodall is late. I sit, dressed and woozy, on a sticky plastic chair in the hospital corridor watching the food carts wobble down the hall. The smell says liver for dinner. I hate liver — I found out by eating it. They've already moved someone else into my room, so she'll have to face it, not me.

Seems all I do is get ordered around. Go here, they say — and I go. Sit there, they say — and I sit. You'll be going home today, they said. And here I am. Waiting to go. Even though I don't know what or where home is.

My hands ache from rubbing them together, and my nails are bitten down as far as they'll go. I hate my hands. Especially when they're wet. Fear makes you sweat, Dr. Browning says. It's okay to be scared, he says. As if by giving me permission to be afraid, the fear will go away. It doesn't.

Sometimes during our sessions I wanted to lean across his desk and smack him as hard as I could. But I didn't. Instead, when he'd say, "Time's up, you can leave now," I'd get up and leave.

His phone number and my appointment time are on a slip of paper in my pocket. But I don't suppose I'll go. A doctor who just shrugs in answer to someone's questions doesn't give that Someone With Traumatic Amnesia much hope. That's what I have. Traumatic Amnesia.

And very little hope.

I stare at the shiny linoleum floor. The smells of overcooked vegetables and sickness swirl around me. I clench my wet hands and tuck them between my knees. I can't stay here and I dread going to the Chalmers-hyphen-Goodalls'.

A pair of scuffed brogues steps into my vision.

"I'm sorry I'm late, Thea," Wilton says. "My car is being temperamental again. And Agatha couldn't get away ... run off her feet, as you know ..."

I pick up my bag and follow him down the hall.

A couple of the nurses wave goodbye as they bustle past. As Wilton and I walk down the concrete stairs, it hits me, with a sickening jolt, that I really am leaving that safe little hole at the end of the second-floor corridor and going out into an unfamiliar world with a stranger who has masking tape holding his glasses together and holes in the elbows of his sweater.

His car is parked near the hospital entrance in a Positively No Stopping zone. A huge uniformed man with a scowl and a clipboard is moving in fast.

No-Action Wilton suddenly comes alive. He throws my bag in amongst a clutter of books in the back and pushes me into the passenger seat. Then he runs around to his side, leaps in and we take off with a roar into heavy traffic. Horns bleat and people make faces at the little car as it weaves back and forth through the traffic. Too late to turn back. Too late to shout stop.

Long white hands grip my knees as if they are the safety rails on my hospital bed. I concentrate on the thin fingers with their short damp nails. Those fingers belong to me. But who am I?

I can hear Dr. Browning's voice echo in my head. *You're going home, Thea. Make the most of it. It will help you remember.*

I look at Wilton's snub-nosed profile. He looks back at me and smiles. My stomach lurches. Do I even *want* to remember?

I grip my knees until I'm sure my bones will crack. I will not sink into the panic that bubbles up into my chest. I won't use the pills Dr. Browning gave me to stop this brain-crushing out-of-control feeling. The tiny tablets make me feel spacey, and there are enough spaces inside me as it is.

The little car swings to the left and rattles along quiet tree-lined streets. Wilton gives me a guided tour. I couldn't care less but try to listen. A voice inside me says, *Concentrate on what he's saying and the panic might stop.*

"Now we've turned toward the river. Even more trees, here, as you can see. And this street – right here – is ours. It's a dead end, really, that stops at the cemetery and church ..."

Dead end. Now *that* makes sense.

"... and we're on the river," Wilton continues.

I want to open the door and leap out screaming. Instead, I wind down my window and try to breathe in some fresh air to calm myself.

"And we get almost no traffic except on Sundays; but as the church is old and, well, Anglican, it's not very busy even then." His chuckle turns into a few dry coughs.

The little car rumbles under a heavy canopy of tall elms. Patterns of sun and shade roll over the hood, and the flickering light through the windshield makes me squint, stretching the stitches on my forehead. This morning a nurse took the large bandage off, and now I have a small flat patch to protect the place where they operated and drained fluid off my brain – along with my memories.

"Here we are." The car comes to a clattering stop in front of a big stone house.

Through my window a thick mist flows in on a gust of wind and clouds my vision. My head swirls with dizziness. There's a faint buzz behind my eyes and a small click inside my head, and the mist and the dizziness disappear as quickly as they came.

"Come along, Thea," Wilton says.

I open the door and get out with slow stiff movements – as if my legs aren't sure how to stand. I look over the top of the car – and suck in a sharp breath.

There it is. Right in front of me.

Home.

I am so surprised, I gasp, "This is it! This is where I lived before the accident."

"Yes ... yes, it is." Wilton smiles suddenly, a genuinely pleased smile. "That's wonderful, Thea. It actually belongs to the church. Remember? Various, uh, clergymen used to live here. We've been renting it for the past — what? — year or so. Do you remember ..."

I stop listening and focus on the gray stone building. Something is wrong. It looks the same and yet it isn't. There's the same huge chimney cutting the facade in two. There's the heavy pilloried stone porch to one side with two rooms above — making it look like the base of a castle tower. All the windows on the front of the house are bowed — just as I remember. And the roof still can't be seen because stone turrets run around the top edge of the walls.

All familiar. But not an exact match. What's missing? What's wrong?

I sag against the car in bewilderment. Shouldn't the trim be a shiny dark green? And why are the window frames and porch rails peeling in heavy curls ready to chip off? As I examine the building, a deep alarm tightens my chest. The longer I look, the less I recognize.

"There shouldn't be hedges in front. Where's the wrought-iron fence? And the — the paint is peeling," I say through dry lips. "And it's such an ugly red."

"Well, actually, there are sections of a metal fence in the hedge. And the paint has been like that since we moved in. We've been meaning to talk to the church elders about repainting it, but we're both so busy ..."

Since they moved in? But it was freshly painted. I chose the colour. Dark green.

Don't think too hard – it hurts. This has to be my home. It doesn't matter about the outside. The inside will be right. I know every corner of every room.

Wilton lowers his voice. "Uh ... Thea, before the others come out to, uh, greet you, I think I should say that we intend not to burden you with too much responsibility right away. And you must not let her, uh, that is *us*, take advantage. That is, well, I don't think Agatha is really *aware,* if you know what I mean. For instance, Agatha and I don't need to take our sabbatical in England this summer. Even though she counted on your looking after the baby when we were gone and ... I know recently you and she were arguing about –"

"Why have you hung blue curtains in my bedroom?" I ask, pointing to the bay window above the porch.

"What? Er, that's not your room, Thea. Your mother – uh, that is, Agatha – and I ... that's our bedroom. We've been there since we moved in. Remember? No, of course you don't. You had your choice of any of the others. You decided on the third-floor bedroom."

I snort. "The attic? You mean Annie's room? I'd never sleep in a servant's room!"

He coughs and his eyes skitter away from mine. "We have no live-in employees, Thea. Certainly no Annie. And if we did we would never use that word – servant. You chose the attic to get some privacy from the other girls. You also said you liked looking down on the garden, which I thought was rather, uh, charming."

The garden. Excitement tightens inside me, like a small but intense light.

"Your mother and the girls have been looking forward to this morning," he says. "Try to be patient with us – it hasn't been easy, if you know what I mean, and –"

Suddenly something he just said pops into my head. "What did you mean about her and me arguing? We didn't argue in the hospital. Did she say we did?"

"Oh no, no. Before the accident, Thea. You and she, well ..." He looks at the house and waves. "There they are!"

Pale faces bob around behind a main-floor window and then withdraw. I shrink back against the car. Oh, god. Thea's sisters.

A few seconds later, four people cram out of the front door. Agatha wears a flowered sun-dress under a checkered flannel shirt and rope sandals. She waddles behind two girls, one about eleven or twelve and the other about four with the face of a tiny wide-eyed monkey. There is also an older woman, hands on her skinny hips and a cigarette hanging out of her mouth. Her hair is the color of the yellow M&Ms Dr. Browning gives to his young patients.

I follow Wilton Goodall. The older girl stares at me as if I have three eyes and a tree growing out of each ear. But the little one throws herself at my legs with a squeal.

"Thea! Thea comed home!"

"These are your sisters, Thea," Agatha says. She spreads

one hand over the head of the tall girl. "This is Electra. We call her Ellie."

The girl is thin and gangly, with a long nose and steel-wool hair tied up in two fuzzy pigtails. Menace glints in the small black eyes.

"You look different," she says.

"Oh dear, this one could be trouble."

Have I spoken out loud? No one reacts, so maybe I just thought it. I try to unhitch the little girl, but she hangs on even tighter.

"Did you bring us a bunch of doctor's needles and stuff? We could play at being nurses," says the one called Ellie.

I shake my head.

"You could just as easily play at being *doctors,* Ellie," Agatha says with a small frown. Her face is shiny and tight, the long upper lip beaded with sweat. "There are lots of women doctors."

Ellie glares at me in disgust.

"And that ... this is Naomi." Agatha points to the girl clinging to my jeans.

"But you always call her Wee." Ellie's black eyes never leave my face.

"Because she's so small?" I ask.

The eyes narrow into slits. "Because she pees her pants and has to wear diapers. You gave her that stupid pathetic name."

"Come on now, Ellie," says Agatha. "A bit more friendly, I think. What's the matter with you? You've been waiting by the window all morning."

"Have not," mumbles the girl.

Wilton coughs and I turn to look at him. Behind him, a tall green hedge shivers and a face appears amongst the tangled leaves. I stare back, but with a faint movement of light it is gone.

If it was there at all.

I haven't been on my feet this long before — not even in the hospital. The broken stone path slowly begins to flap up and down.

"Okay, you lot," says the woman on the stairs. "Out of the way. The kid's about to drop. Come on inside, Thea. I'm Germaine. I clean house here. You'll remember me quick enough." Her smile is a knowing smirk.

Agatha drags the protesting Wee off me and dutifully follows Germaine into the house. I concentrate on keeping my feet from sinking through the spongy path. Wilton helps me up the shifting stairs.

As soon as we cross the threshold, I hear a voice — chiding and intimate. "For heaven's sake, girl, get a grip on yourself or you'll be no use to me at all." A light laugh stirs the hair on the nape of my neck.

A girl's voice. My own? I don't recognize it. There is no one behind Wilton and he doesn't seem to have heard it. First a face in the hedge, and now I'm hearing voices. I straighten up and try to concentrate. The hallway does have some familiar furniture in it, but everything else is wrong.

"What has become of the grandfather clock and the

corner cabinet here in the vestibule?" someone asks. "Those fixtures are church property. Who removed them? And the Oriental rug?" This time I recognize my voice, hanging in the air, distant and fuzzy. But I don't know where the questions came from. Wilton's hand, under my elbow, tightens.

"We don't have no such *fixtures* in the *vestibule*," Ellie says, "so we can't tell you what has *become* of them." Her face looms right in front of mine and she says loudly, "Why is she talking funny? Hey, she looks weird. Her eyes are kind of crossed. Gone nuts from that hit on the head?"

"Never you mind," says the one called Germaine. "Stick her in the living room and I'll pour us all some lemonade."

I feel better sitting down. I look around the big room. The marble fireplace has a pile of books where the grate should be and the brass peacock fire-screen is missing. Two old couches are covered in tattered shawls. Threadbare rugs overlap on the worn wood floors. More books stand in piles along the walls. The green-and-cream striped wallpaper is stained and dingy. On two small rectory tables are more books, dusty bric-a-brac, and squat earthenware pots filled with dried grasses and dying plants.

"What's happened?" I ask in wonder. "The parlor's gone to ruin. How did all this rubbish get in here? And where is the –"

I stop talking when I see the sidelong glances they are giving each other. The little girl, Wee, tries to climb up on me. I push her down gently. After a few more tries she gives up, gropes her thumb into her mouth and lowers her head to my lap.

She smells strongly of ammonia and her hair is all tatty. I lean away from her and try to ignore the sticky fingers patting my hand. It's strange – I have a vague recollection of those tiny monkey fingers, but I am too busy trying to figure out this room.

It's wrong. All, all wrong. A flutter of panic makes my heart skip a few beats.

I have a very clear image of what this room should look like. Where is the rest of the solid plain furniture, the regimented rows of books in tall glass-fronted bookshelves, the porcelain and bronze ornaments on the mantelpiece? And where is the painting?

"What are you looking for?" Agatha asks. "I don't think anything's been changed since you went in the hospital."

I point to the large faded square on the wallpaper over the fireplace. "What has become of my portrait?"

All eyes follow my finger.

Silence falls like smoke around the room.

"Her portrait. She's asking about a picture, right?" the one called Ellie whispers eagerly. "Like we'd actually have a picture of *her* up there."

"We've never had a painting there, Thea," Agatha says patiently, as if talking to an idiot. "We've always planned to fill that space with one of your watercolors, but you haven't – hadn't – found exactly what you wanted. Maybe you *planned* a self-portrait."

Somewhere, deep inside, I sense a dim memory of a different way of being – one in which I know exactly who

I am and what I'm doing. Colors swirl in my head, dragged around by huge paintbrushes with soft fat bristles.

I am unprepared when, from out of nowhere, a huge gray cat drops onto my lap. A starburst of shock jolts me back to earth.

"That's Purvice," Ellie says. "Do you remember Purr?"

I stare at the cat, my fingertips tingling. Wee strokes his tail and throbbing chuckles vibrate the animal's whole body. He bats his big head softly against my arm.

"No," I say, finally, through dry lips. "I don't remember a cat."

The animal puts his paws on my shoulders and raises his head level with mine, studying me without blinking. I gaze into his slanted yellow eyes. Why don't I remember him? I am about to lift my hand to pat him when out of his mouth comes a crackling hiss. Needle-sharp claws dig into my skin. I sweep him and the girl off me and leap to my feet.

The room slides out of focus. Something squeezes my head so tightly I can't think. The people and the dingy walls press closer. The air is oppressive and hot. It's as if I am dust and heat, and any moment I will scatter and disappear.

I manage to whisper, "I have to lie down. I can find my own way."

I walk carefully and quickly out of the room.

CHAPTER FOUR

I hear them gabbling behind me. But I keep right on going, past the dining room, past Papa's study — I don't dare look in — and up the stairs.

"Thea! Wait!"

The whole Dreadful Crew is gathered below. I want to laugh at the looks on their faces. Words come to mind — face-smacked, stunned. Mouths gaping.

I remember Papa saying, *Close it, my dear, or the flies will move in and take up housekeeping.*

I remember?

Germaine holds a loaded tea tray, the smoldering cigarette stuck to her bottom lip. Agatha pulls at the ripped pocket of her shirt, her face screwed up.

Who is Papa?

The girls stand together at the bottom of the staircase, eyes wide, while Wilton edges up the treads very slowly, as if trying not to startle me. I want to shout, "Boo!" into his face, but I don't have the energy. In the dim light his eyes are enlarged and blurred behind the thick lenses.

"Do I call you Papa?" I ask him.

He looks puzzled. "Er … no. Sometimes Dad, usually Wilton – but if you'd like to call me Papa … if it, uh, feels right for you –"

"It's okay. Just asking." The dizziness suddenly returns and I sit down hard on the top stair.

"Thea? Are you okay?"

I can only nod, because I am watching a cloud form in front of my eyes. I squeeze them shut and open them again quickly. It's still there, but it slides away to hang in the air behind Wilton's shoulder. A voice, familiar and unknown, breathes out of the thickening haze.

"He's lost to me. Find him. Find him for me."

Wilton follows my wide-eyed gaze. The gray curtain shimmers and dissolves.

"Did you see – hear that?" I ask him.

"See what? Hear what?" His eyes grow enormous with concern. "I think you're rather overtired, Thea. Can I help you up?"

I can't move. A dreadful certainty pounds in my head. I *am* seeing things that aren't there. The face in the hedge and now this. And I *am* hearing voices that don't exist, that no one else can hear. I gasp for air, but I breathe in hot dry dust.

"I – I –"

"She's going to be sick!" Germaine shouts up to us. "Get her to the can – quick!"

I throw up three times into a stained toilet. Wilton Goodall stays in the hall, just out of sight, asking me if I'm okay over and over in a loud whisper.

"Oh, shut up. Please!" I finally snap.

In the blissful silence I wash my face. My throat and head hurt. I just want a bed to lie on, with a soft pillow for my pounding head.

On phantom limbs I walk down the hall. Wilton smiles an apology at me, his face a light greenish tinge. Behind us, at the end of the dark hall, the rest of the Dreadful Crew has gathered. Agatha walks up to us pulling on the sleeve of her flannel shirt. I hear a faint tearing sound.

She and Wilton show me a stairway at the end of the second-floor corridor. Agatha flicks a switch, which lights up walls covered in misty green paintings stuck on drab wallpaper. I stare. Every painting is a small section of the garden of my dreams.

"Who did these?"

"You did," Wilton says. "You loved to paint the garden."

"It became almost an obsession," Agatha adds.

I stumble up the stairs past images that blur into a green jungle of trees and bushes touched here and there with splotches of mauve, white and blue. The landing turns out to be a tiny hallway, also covered with paintings, broken by one narrow door. Wilton squeezes past and opens it. He and Agatha stand back and let me go in first.

The low-ceilinged room is filled with streaks of yellow light coming from a single large window. Beside it crouches a huge bed with claw feet and a carved headboard. Somehow I expected a plain metal bed frame. Why do I remember this room belonging to a maid called Annie?

Yet I know this bed. They must have carried it and the other dark furniture up here when I was in the hospital. I finger my bandage. It's as if little glimmers of memory are somewhere in the crackling electricity in my head but they fly past too quickly to hold on to.

Above the bed, around the window and across the walls are more frameless paintings. All of a large tangled garden. Layers of gossamer fabrics in hazy pastels – watered silks and embroidered chiffons – have been pinned all across the ceiling. They swirl above and drift down the walls like pale leaves and drooping petals – a tent of dusty rainbow cobwebs.

"Was this Thea's ... that is, *my* room?"

"Yes. Yes, it was – is your room," Agatha says.

"Who did this?" I ask, pointing up.

Wilton looks bewildered. "Why, you did."

Agatha adds with a smile, "Your allowance went on them. We wondered about it, but we didn't – don't – want to crush your creativity, so of course ..."

The single window has no curtain or shade, just a fine bug screen behind the glass. If I look out will I see the garden from my dreams? Beautiful trees and trimmed hedges and lush flowers?

I hear a faint sound – like the hiss of air through someone's teeth – and in my head a faint pop. My eyes blur and then clear again in a split second; but my legs feel unbelievably heavy, just like when I got out of the car.

Slowly, I walk to the window. For a moment I think I can see the faint reflection of a girl with long hair standing directly behind my shoulder, but just as our eyes meet, she dissolves and my own image stares back at me. I squeeze my eyes shut and press my forehead against the coolness of the pane. I'm afraid to look outside in case I see something else that isn't really there.

I open my eyes slowly. And there it is. The Garden. Under the trees, the shadows are dark green and cool as water. But like the rest of this house, it isn't right. The tall shiny-leafed hedges that outline the area all the way to the river are unrestrained and wild, not neatly clipped. Beyond those hedges, however, the river shines like polished pewter in the afternoon light. At least that hasn't changed.

But everything else is wrong, wrong, wrong! The whisper echoes in my head. The pond, rather than sparkling at the far end of the yard, is ochre brown and stagnant behind scraggly bushes. I can barely make out its limestone border — covered as it is with weeds and thick humps of grass.

The three apple trees I planted when we moved in are in full bloom, their twisted, gnarled trunks covered with thin trails of acid-green vines. A breeze scatters a handful of their petals across the wide expanse of knee-high grass.

In the flower beds, regiments of nettles, horsetails and thistles rise above the choked perennials like the straight-backed soldiers of an invading army.

How — how could this have happened? All my hard work wasted.

"How long have I been away?"

Agatha says, "Just about a month. You know that."

"I know only what I've been told."

They're lying. They must be. As I stare at the garden, uncomprehending rage mounts inside me. It would take years for it to become so overgrown. Years? How many? I'm — Thea is — only sixteen years old. Could she — I — possibly have planted these aging crusted trees? A surge of panic flushes through me, making my stomach hurt and my fingers tingle. I take slow deep breaths, like Dr. Browning taught me. I have to concentrate, to ask The Parents the right questions. There has to be a reasonable explanation for thinking it was me who planted everything in the garden. I am about to turn away from the window when I sense a faint shifting of light and shadow under one of the basswood trees close to the neighbor's hedge.

Someone is in the garden.

Another flutter of shadows and a face appears, floating around the tree trunk. It's gone so quickly I can't tell if it was the same face I saw in the hedge by the front door. Deep inside the tree's shadow I see more furtive movement, followed by a quiver of branches in the hedge farther down. And then stillness.

Am I imagining this — like the mist on the stairs? Like the faint figure in the window? Too many questions. Too much to think about. Exhaustion overpowers me and I sink onto the bed.

The downstairs rooms were warm from the late-spring sunshine. This room, so near the roof, should be even warmer. But it's icy cold. Soon my whole body is shuddering with it.

Maybe if I just rest awhile … just awhile …

Someone covers me with a silky comforter.

Wilton's voice comes from a long way off. "The doctor told us it would take some time, didn't he? This shouldn't cause any immediate worry … should it?"

Agatha's voice is impatient. "How do I know? She seems okay. Just tired. Let her rest. Look, I have a meeting in half an hour, so I've got to run. Thea? Do you need one of those little white pills? Or a painkiller? Ellie can get it for you. She's been quite a good help since you've been gone, although I must say she's easily distracted. What would you like?"

I can't answer.

"A pill or not?"

I shake my head and wrap the cover tightly around me. My whole body aches from fighting – fear, pain, disappointment, the cold inside and around me. I just want Thea's parents to go away. I can hear them whispering and then, far away, the click of the door as it shuts.

The sun spreads over the cover. Under its warmth, my shaking stops and I suddenly feel very light. I am drifting on a thin skim of air – like floating on water.

A girl's voice – in my head? right beside my ear? – says, "You poor girl. What am I going to do with you now?"

Who is it? Is she talking to me? I struggle to think, but I am lifted higher on the warm air. Then, with a sickening lurch, I spiral down into smothering blackness.

CHAPTER FIVE

I know he is waiting. He will be by the silvery fountain. Despite the danger my heart is light and full, like the pale shell of the moon that hangs in the ink-washed sky.

There he is – in the shadow of the tall cedars. I run toward him. "Thus I set my printless feet o'er the cowslip's velvet head, that bends not as I tread." I recite Milton's words to the warm darkness and laugh with joy. Then I stumble, and the damp ground dissolves under my feet. I hear him call, "Susannah!", but I am plummeting through icy emptiness.

I wake up with a violent jolt.

The light in the room is a misty somber blue. A shaky glance at my watch says five-thirty. I've slept for over twelve hours. I'm still in the clothes I wore home from the hospital. My back is damp with sweat and there is a light weight against it. I turn my head as far as I can and peer over my shoulder. Wee is under the covers, curled up like a tiny mouse.

Something soft swishes across my face. The cat is stretched out between me and the headboard, his tail trailing back and forth contentedly. So he's decided he's not afraid of me after all. Between the two of them, I'm crammed against the wall.

Disappointment stabs me. I'll never get back to sleep again — to the danger and sweetness of that dream. Who was I running toward? Why did he call out "Susannah"? Why call *me* Susannah?

I'm being silly. It was just a dream. Dreams don't mean anything. I sit up and sneeze. It doesn't wake the sleeping mouse-child and my head doesn't roll off my shoulders, so I slither out and sit on the end of the bed.

The window is hazy and blue, as if the world outside hasn't taken on a definite shape yet. I feel like that, too — formless and vague.

Panic squeezes my chest. Why doesn't anything feel concrete and firm and ... real? Concentrate. One thing at a time. Get up. Get dressed.

Someone must have carried my bag up when I was sleeping. It lies open on the floor beside a dresser that supports a big dusty mirror. Next to the dresser stands a tall wooden wardrobe with crackled brown varnish. As quietly as I can, I open its doors.

I paw through hanger after hanger of dark clothes. Good grief. Didn't Thea have any imagination? But then I find the dresser drawers are jammed with bracelets, pierced earrings and cheap rings of every shape and design and color, while all over the top of the dresser are bottles of cream and little plastic cases of gray and pink and copper eye shadows and tubes of blood-red lipsticks. What on earth must she have looked like with her scarlet lips and black clothes?

The wooden surface of the dresser is marked with nail-polish drops, stains and pale blotches where the varnish has been water-damaged. And dust everywhere. Thick dust. A careless girl. Even so, her family might have bothered to clean up for her homecoming.

On the other side of the dresser is a small table covered in painting supplies — two pickle jars stuffed with brushes, a stack of thick paper and one box filled with little tubes smeared with colors — Cadmium, Prussian Blue, Titanium White and Vermilion. Another box is jammed with pastels, pencils, erasers and more tubes of paint. A drinking glass has a paintbrush standing head down in thick sludge. The bristles will be ruined. Beside the glass is a page covered in a thin wash of green.

I finger the tubes of paint. A faint memory stirs and flutters away. I stand in the half-light and peer earnestly into the dresser's streaky mirror. In the hospital I examined every inch of that face — looking for something familiar. When the swelling around my eyes and face finally went down I'd hoped to recognize something. But I didn't.

Now I see the same strange oval with its wide pale forehead, large brown eyes, straight eyebrows, thin slice of nose and shiny wings of black hair sticking out around the white bandage.

"Who are you?" I whisper.

No one answers. I stare gloomily at the belongings of the girl I'm supposed to be. This isn't making me feel better. Action before misery, right, Dr. Browning?

I throw my creased and soiled clothes onto the wardrobe floor and pull on clean underwear, a pair of shorts and a long black T-shirt with a pale gold sun design on it. I strap on leather sandals, smiling down at my pale thin toes. With my bare feet and legs I feel strangely free. I seem to remember thick-soled shoes that lace up high over heavy white stockings, yet there are no white stockings or shoes in the wardrobe or drawers.

I grab a sterile bandage and my washing things and am halfway across the room when I realize the air is icy cold, even though the window is shut. Slowly, as if a breeze is washing through them, the cobwebby fabrics above me flutter and undulate. I grip my toothbrush so tightly the bristles prick the palm of my hand.

The bedroom door creaks open.

"Who's there?" My voice is a high squeak. A flicker of white, like the edge of an apron, flashes on the other side of the door. Without thinking I call, "Annie? Is that you?"

No one answers. There is no white-aproned servant named Annie in this house. Wilton said so. I am imagining things again.

The sleeping girl doesn't stir, but the cat slinks to the end of the bed, staring at the open door. With a low growl, tail straight up, feet a blur, he disappears into the dark safety of the wardrobe. What did *he* see out in the hall?

The feeling of being watched leaves as quickly as it came. I let out my breath with a soft *whumph*. Should I wake the little girl? No. Leave her. She's okay where she is and I can't bear the way she clings to me. I peer out into the short hall. Keep calm. It was probably the other sister sneaking around. Concentrate on finding the bathroom.

My sick mess appears to have been washed away but it would hardly matter. Wet towels lie in heaps on the floor, a soggy plastic diaper is snagged on the edge of a garbage pail, and the sink is splattered with blobs of toothpaste and slivers of soap. Mould grows like a fuzzy rash all along the tile above the claw-footed tub.

These people have destroyed every room in the house. The bathroom was always so orderly, so clean, so – I search for the word – discreet. Papa and I always timed our visits so that we wouldn't meet each other in our night attire. I rub the bandage on my forehead. Where have the memories of a tidy bathroom come from? This bathroom can't have seen an orderly moment since the Chalmers-Goodalls moved in.

And if this Papa person is not Wilton who could he be? Before the sliver of panic burrows deeper in my chest, I quickly wash my face, replace the bandage and leave.

Downstairs, the hallway leads to a door covered in tattered green felt. From behind it comes a loud clatter followed by equally loud curses.

I open the swinging door to find Germaine chasing a whirling pot lid across the ceramic floor. I put out my foot.

Both noises stop. I lift the lid from under my sandal and hand it to her.

"So you're up, are you?" she says around a drooping cigarette. "I'm not ready to serve yet, and I don't make special breakfasts, either. You hate porridge and we're outta bread."

"I'm sure I can manage, thank you. Are you always here so early?"

"Six A.M. to two o'clock now, so I can still be home in time to get Herbert fed before bingo starts. Now you're back I'll come in at nine again pretty soon."

"Herbert. Your husband?"

"Herbert's my spaniel, missy, and you know it!" She slams the lid on a pot of bubbling glop. "I'll be glad when you stop this crap and get back to making their breakfasts again. It isn't my job."

"It doesn't look as if you *have* a job, if the state of the bathroom is anything to go by." I can't seem to stop myself. I decide she is a dark mustard yellow. Sharp, murky and harsh.

"Well, pardon me, Miss Hoity-toity," she sneers.

Horrible old woman. I'll have to speak to Papa when I — a shaft of pain slides behind my left eye as a round face topped by silver hair inches into my memory. The thick features are twisted with rage. All around me a whisper hisses, louder and louder, until it forms understandable words. "... a day's work yourself, you lazy girl ... dreaming about in that garden of yours when I need your help with the parish work. Mark me well ... in works of labor or of skill, I would be busy, too, for Satan finds mischief still, for idle hands to do ... idle ..."

"No!" a voice cries. "Not him! Not him!"

I clamp my hands over my ears to block the voices out. "Stop it!"

"Eh? What's that?" Germaine looks at me intently. "I don't figure you got any right to tell me to *stop* anything!"

"I — I didn't mean you." I concentrate on the table instead. Bowls, cups and spoons are stacked beside a pot of honey, a carton of juice and a plate of fat plain crackers, each as big as my hand. With trembling fingers I smear one with butter. It tastes like salty cardboard.

Germaine eyes me up and down. "So how come there's no 'back from the dead' makeup? No black eye shadow? No gooey red lipstick? Is this a new 'pale stranger' routine you've worked out?"

"She always wore a lot of makeup?" I ask, remembering the pile of cosmetics on the dresser.

"*She* always wore? What's that supposed to mean? *She* is *you!* What kind of a question is that?"

"A simple one, surely."

"You know very well *you* wore gobs of it. A different face for every new little drama you worked up. I suppose this bare-faced look is to prove you don't *remember* walking around looking like someone from 'The Twilight Zone.'"

"What's that?"

She puts hands on skinny hips. The ash from her

cigarette falls to the floor.

"You can't fool me, Theadora Chalmers-Goodall —"

"With a hyphen," I mutter.

"You're putting on this act so those two don't take off for the summer, aren't you? You told me you were fed up being their built-in cook and baby-sitter. You said you'd find a way out. Come on, you can tell me — I won't blab."

The door from the hallway bangs open and Ellie walks in, dressed in a light blue tracksuit with dirty knees.

"Must be nice, huh? Skipping classes, staying home." Her thin-lipped smile irritates me.

"Just be glad you have somewhere to go," I snap.

"Yeah. Any place is better than this, right? That's what you used to say. Now here you are, stuck until summer holidays. Hah! By then I bet you'll decide to get your memory back."

Germaine grins. "See? You may have fooled your parents and the doctors, but not Ellie and me. They didn't hear you grumbling on about getting away from all the work around here."

Angry words enter my head. "How dare you suggest that I am making this up! If you don't watch your tongue, you'll find yourself on the street without a job. Papa won't tolerate such insolence."

She snorts. "Not bad. But a little bit *too* uppity to be convincing. And as for your 'papa,' Wilton Goodall hasn't a clue ..."

Ellie mimics me. "Papa won't tolerate such insolence.

Jeez, you sound weirder and weirder. Who's this Papa guy? It sure isn't Daddy."

"I am not talking about your father," I sneer, then bite my tongue.

"Oh really? He's not just *my* father, dummy-face. You're so stupid, you know that? Act stupid. Look stupid —"

"Okay, that's enough," says Germaine. "Ellie, go and wake up your little sister."

Ellie glares at us, then bangs the door open with the flat of her hand.

She may have a nasty mouth, but she's right. Who am I talking about? The dim shape of the silver-haired man slides forward, but before I can grab hold, it draws back into its dark cave. Confused, I stare at Germaine. Does she — does everyone in the house — know who this Papa person is? Are they just not telling me? Germaine stares defiantly back, but her self-satisfied smile becomes uncertain and slips sideways off her face. Slowly she takes the cigarette stub out of her mouth.

"Thea?"

I turn and walk quickly out the back door, into the damp and tangled garden, past leafy ferns, past overgrown lilac bushes with sparse blossoms and faint peppery smells, past the slimy water of the pond, with its ring of mossy stones and brackish stink, toward the thick hedges that rim the yard.

Everything out here is still *all wrong*. To see the house so run-down is bad enough, but the garden makes my heart ache. How could it have gone from the sweeping lawns, elegantly trimmed rosebushes, tall dahlias, larkspur, Canterbury bells, day lilies and other lush perennials I see in my dreams to this horrible mess? And in barely four weeks? It simply could not have happened. It must be longer. It has to be. If so, where have I *been?*

The Parents, the whole Dreadful Crew, *must* be lying about how long ago the accident happened, if an accident happened at all. They must be lying about everything. Maybe even about who they are.

As I look around, another image forms in my mind — two girls playing hide-and-seek in this same ruined garden, circling the pond and swirling through the grass, shrieking like gulls. A taller girl with black hair chases them with echoing whoops and cries.

Prickles run up and down my arms. Thea's two sisters. And me.

A faint breeze lifts my hair and whispers, "*Susannah. I am here.*"

Who am I? Who?

CHAPTER SIX

"Thea!"

Germaine's shrill voice follows me down the long garden, but I duck into a gap in the hedge. Squeezing through the narrow opening, I leave full sunshine and emerge into the deep shade of a churchyard, where enormous elms entwine overhead into a single green canopy.

To my right, a stone church with a pointed steeple stands behind a row of lilacs. To my left, sun-splashed bushes line the riverbank. Across the water's wide expanse, the distant bank rises like a sandy wall. Above it I can see more trees with men working in their branches, chain saws droning like angry bees. Cars flash by on a faraway road, and now and again a cyclist zips along a path near the water's edge.

Right in front of me is a shadowy cemetery surrounded by a crooked iron fence with pointed spikes at regular intervals. When I pass through a little foot gate, the air around me shifts, changes, as if the graveyard doesn't belong to the sunny busy world across the river.

In that muted bubble, birds twitter lazily, making everything seem more still. I move through damp coolness, crunching along narrow paths between black earth rectangles with concrete borders and elaborately carved headstones. A few graves have been planted with flowers, pale and sickly in the gloomy light.

Reading the inscriptions on the headstones keeps my mind from scattering like the tiny flies that rise with every footstep. A memory of doing this before drifts into my mind, but I push it away. It doesn't matter. Nothing matters.

When I die, who will they bury? An old woman named Thea whose memory didn't begin until she was sixteen? Or will it be someone else — someone named Susannah?

As if an invisible hand has appeared in front of me, I stop beside a small spreading tree. The lowest branches just reach the top of my head. I step into its inky shadow and feel its pointed leaves brush my hair. It's so dark I move forward cautiously, but my foot catches on something and I land hard on my knees. Directly in front of me is the bottom half of a shiny marble headstone, the top half lying face down beside it. Rubbing each knee in turn, I lean closer to the stone. There is only a date: 1929.

As soon as my fingers touch the cool marble, the sun flashes like a strobe through the leaves and I am flying forward at a great speed, hair whipping around my head, wind roaring in my ears. A shout echoes above me. I look up to discover that the tree is still there, its flapping branches splattering me with seeds and twigs. I haven't moved at all.

Through a yellow mist just ahead, someone is coming toward me. A girl on a bike, eyes smoky with makeup, lips bright red, legs pumping hard on the pedals, bike wheels taking the sharp turns in the gravel path with ease.

It's *her!*

I have to stop her. She can't go sailing by, ducking her head when she passes under the tree's branches as she does every day. Not this time. The cold wind presses me toward the earth, but I pull myself high enough to grab a branch and drag it down. Not to hurt her, just to stop her.

Suddenly I am on the bike, pedaling furiously, trying to sort out how I will confront my mother about her trip to England. I can't be left alone all summer looking after – out of nowhere, someone stands up under my usual short-cut tree.

It's a girl with long hair. She raises a white hand and pulls one of the branches down, barring my way. I veer to avoid hitting it but I turn too late. Something slams into my head.

I lie on the ground – unhurt, no bike, no one near – and stare up at the tangled leaves, my mind a muddle of bewilderment and relief.

Think. If it was me – Thea – on that bike, how could I see her – me – so clearly, as if I was a spectator? How could I be in two places at once? There's no answer. Unless I'm crazy.

Is that what's happening?

I sit up. Concentrate. Count the headstones. One, two, three ... My mind slows down. Four, five ... six ... seven. That gray marble one is eight, the pinkish stone is nine, the black one is ten. Eleven is a tall very grand monument covered in silver plaques, which sits alone in a graveled octagon, paths radiating from it. On the top is the stone figure of a young man, sitting cross-legged. I stop counting and focus on it.

Odd. Why would a sculptor put a hat on the long-haired figure? Ah, it's a real hat, somebody's idea of a joke. Wait! The statue moved – I'm sure of it – a small shift in the shoulders as if easing tension.

In fact, isn't the whole statue dressed in real clothes? Underneath the gray tweed jacket the shirt is a dull white and, yes, that's the silvery-blue of washed-out jeans. The narrow chin rests on folded hands, the elbows on bent knees. And the shadowed eyes are looking at me.

I scramble to my feet. For a split second my view is blocked by an overhanging branch. When I push it aside, the "statue" is gone. In its place is a plain stone cross. All is quiet. No movement. No sound.

I *am* definitely seeing things that aren't there. What is the name for this? Hallucinating. Yes, I'm hallucinating. That explains how I can see myself in two places at once and how a statue can come alive and then vanish.

I touch my arms and legs to make sure I am actually in one piece, not floating in little bits through the leaves of the trees like the flies that dance around my head. I'm sticky with sweat. The air is suffocatingly hot. It's hard to breathe, hard to think.

A hissing sound, very faint yet penetrating, rises from the ground behind me. I leap to my feet and race away over the gravel paths, back through the gap in the hedge and across the long grass toward the house.

I stop on the back stoop, holding a stitch in my side. I need time alone to sort things out by myself. Suddenly, laughter bubbles up – harsh and loud in the heavy air. I've done it again. Used that word. *Myself*. Will I know who myself is before they cart me off to the loony-bin?

CHAPTER SEVEN

I sneak through the back door, the wound under the bandage pulsing against my skull. It only hurts when I laugh out loud, Dr. Browning. I should take one of those pink painkillers and lie down.

Milky puddles, dirty bowls, half-filled glasses and cups are strewn over the crumb-scattered tabletop. The house is quiet. With any luck the whole Crew's eaten and gone.

But no. I bump into Agatha and the little kid in the hall. Agatha grabs my arm and drags me into the living room talking a mile a minute. Wee gets a death grip on one of my legs. It's hard concentrating with a mouse-girl snuffling into your T-shirt.

"Naomi, love, go out and wait for me in the car," Agatha says. Under her eyes are dark mauve smudges that match the purple flowered top stretched across her big stomach. "Now, Thea —"

"When is this one due?" I press the bandage with my fingertips to ease the ache in my head.

She looks startled. "In about a month. Why?"

"Will you stay home then? Look after the kids?"

"Don't start, Thea. We've been through this again and again. You know that your father and I see the family unit as a small community. Each person has jobs to do. Team-work, you know. You also know that we're deliberately teaching you girls different skills, skills you can apply to the world outside the home – community skills, administration skills –"

I snort. "Ellie's only eleven years old. Wee can't even talk properly."

"I *know* that, thank you, Thea. But Ellie can do many things in our family unit, *did* do them while you were in hospital. But I must say, she's changed. Become more like you – snarky, unco-operative, even belligerent. It's very disappointing. Your father and I are attempting to create a well-oiled machine. If we all pull our weight it's so efficient that everyone gets to do their own thing, too. Like your paintings, or your father's teaching or *my* work – which happens to be extremely vital."

Is she kidding? Not a glint of humor in those dark blue eyes.

"But what do *you* do around here – in the house, I mean?" I ask. "Do you look after Wee? No, according to Germaine that's Thea's job. Do you look after Ellie? No, that's Thea's – my – job, too. Wilton informed me that I do the shopping and banking. And apparently I do breakfasts and dinners and lunches."

"We all do our part, miss. Which means your father and I earn the money that keeps you in paints and makeup. I work hard, believe me."

"At what?"

"At wha– ? Oh. Right. It's hard to remember that you can't ..." she shrugs "... remember." Then she begins to speak slowly, as if to a child. "I teach psychology at the university. I also have private clients and workshops – like my fear-of-pregnancy groups – and I'm trying to start a Samaritans program at the university. It's a British concept – volunteers counselling people by phone." She runs a puffy hand over her mop of hair. "That's why we're hoping to go to England this summer. Samaritans research. I am needed everywhere – everywhere at once! So you and everyone else in this house have to pull – "

"Their weight. Yes. I think I've figured that out, thanks."

Wee, who hasn't moved an inch since Agatha ordered her out of the room, starts to whine loudly.

"Naomi!" Agatha snaps. "I told you to wait in the car."

Wee's face is a mask of misery, but she stays put.

"Where exactly are you taking her?" I ask.

Agatha looks at Wee accusingly. "Ignore the theatrics, Thea. Lately she's been acting as if I'm dragging her off to a torture chamber. I'm driving her to day care for the morning, that's all. In the afternoon she goes to Sunny Days Nursery School."

"What's the matter with her? Why does she talk like she does? And isn't she too old for diapers? Is she retarded?"

"No! Good heavens no. Thea, psychologists do not employ that word anymore. In any case it's not relevant in regards to Naomi. Wilton's brother was just like Wee and he's a lawyer now. Her problems are not anything that'll hold her back for long. She's just regressed a little since your accident, that's all."

"Regressed?"

"You were helping with her language and reading, and she's forgotten some of the learning strategies you developed for her. She's gone back to less complex language skills, and she's been unable to connect with Ellie on her reading. You were also working, under my guidance, on developing her socialization skills before kindergarten starts. But it was her reading that you were concentrating on the most."

"Don't you ever read to her?"

"Me? I have no time to keep up in my own field, let alone ... Besides, you ..." She looks uncomfortable.

"I do it all."

Wee grips my leg tighter.

"Looks like you've got to obey your mother," I say to the sad little face. "But I'll see you later, all right?"

In her croaky voice she says, "You goed away. Outside. You said no. I look for you. You gone. You no go away again."

"Don't worry. I just went for a walk before breakfast. Now I'm going to lie down. I've been sick, remember? I'll see you tonight."

She gives this serious thought, then nods solemnly. "See you at home. No go on bike. No *go*. Okay?"

"No, I won't go on my bike."

Satisfied, she leaves the room dragging a chewed-up

blanket that might once have been pink.

When I glance at Agatha her face is flushed. "You have to understand, Thea, that —"

"Where's Ellie?"

She sighs. "Wilton drove her to school. She's in a spring play, and rehearsals are at seven-thirty." She glances at her watch and lets out a little scream. "Is that the time?"

She grabs two loaded briefcases, staggers toward the door and is gone.

I sit down on the couch, choked with anger, but the door opens again and her salt-and-pepper mop reappears. "I'll see you later, Thea. Take some time to regroup, okay? Some personal quality time. We'll, um, talk later, okay?"

The door closes again. I'm surprised when tears burn my eyes. But they're not just for me. They're for that *other* Thea. The one Agatha wants back — but for her own selfish reasons, not for Thea's sake.

As soon as I hear the rumble of the car engine I make for the stairs. I will not let Agatha upset me. She's in for a big surprise if she thinks *I'm* going to be the nanny and cook around here.

A vacuum cleaner starts up in one of the bedrooms, loud thumps accompanying the grumbles of the operator. It appears that Germaine manages to do *something* now and again. Surprisingly, when I reach the stairs to the third floor my headache has eased. I climb slowly, looking at the paintings.

They're all of the garden — the way it is now — overgrown and scruffy, the pond dark and murky. Then where does the memory come from — of a crystal-clear pond filled with gold and silver black-spotted fish? And why can I see in my mind's eye, high above them, the spray of a fountain, blowing circles of fine mist? One of the paintings makes me hesitate. Is that a figure hovering behind a stand of pale hollyhocks? When I concentrate on it, the figure changes into odd shapes of light and disappears.

A girl. With long hair. Like the girl in the window? Like the girl in the cemetery?

I run up the rest of the stairs, close the bedroom door behind me and look anywhere but at the paintings on the walls. I can feel their energy all around me, calling me to look. To look closely. I should take them down, throw them away.

Was Thea so lonely that this was all she could do? Paint the garden over and over? Was this her only escape? I can't help but wonder if she was okay in the head even before the accident.

Maybe when I get my memory back I'll find out she was nuts all along. I? She? I stifle a giggle that, if it explodes, will be shrill and frightening in the still bubble of air that surrounds me.

I clench my fists and tuck them between my knees to try to stop the dread building inside me. Dr. Browning kept saying that something in my life might have played a part in my memory loss, and that once I find out what it is I will start getting better. Could he be right? *Is* there something?

What could have made Thea want to escape her world? Did she spend too much time daydreaming about a better place and end up tangled in a fantasy somehow? Is that why I'm hearing voices and seeing things that aren't really here? Have the things that Thea — I mean, *I* — daydreamed before the accident magically come to life? A possible answer jabs at me like a tiny poisoned needle.

I'm just plain crazy.

No! Thea was not crazy. I'm not crazy. I won't allow it. I have to stay in control. I have to be sensible, like Dr. Browning says. Yet right now, I seem to be caught in a hollow unknown space filled with terrifying sounds and sights. Panic explodes like a starburst in my chest. Stop. Concentrate on something else.

One step at a time. Stay in control. Willpower. All it takes is willpower. I start to pace — back and forth, back and forth.

I'm afraid to go into the garden. If I go downstairs, I'll probably bump into Germaine, and if I stay in this room with nothing to do I'll go even crazier. What can I do? Right now, this very minute. What can I do?

My eyes stop at the painting table.

I pick up a crockery plate shaped like a daisy, and with trembling fingers quickly squeeze a different color into each spoon-shaped petal. Then I grab a stack of papers and the glass of water from my night table and sit cross-legged on the end of the bed beside the window. From up here, I'm able to see the entire Chalmers-Goodall yard and the back half of the neighbor's. If I can't go into the garden, maybe I can paint it — like Thea did.

It comes naturally, as if someone else is mixing the colors. I take a clean brush and wash the top sheet of paper with water. Then I slide a mixture of blue and gray through the wetness, leaving spaces here and there for clouds. I mix a darker gray for them and try to capture their rolling movement across the sky.

The scene outside my window is bathed in the unreal radiance of dark thundery skies mixed with splashes of bright sunshine on powdery blossoms. A faint breath of weedy pond water and grassy earth drifts in on the breeze, contrasting with warm stale air and the smell of paint.

I work quickly, and the scene outside reappears on my paper like magic. Using drier brushes, I swirl white and blue and hints of green and yellow. I add more gray, then a splash of cream and a touch of dusky brown. I set that painting aside and start another. And another when that one is complete.

Soon three paintings are spread out in a half circle around me, the garden lying like a watery shadow across each page – not the tangled garden of Thea's paintings, but three views of a formal garden with groomed hedges, flower beds of vibrant colors and wide clipped lawns.

A tingling shiver skitters up my arms when I look closely at the last painting. Somehow my brushes have painted a girl standing in front of the fountain's spray.

Her back is to the house, her head half turned, looking toward the neighbor's – as if listening. Who is it? It can't be me. Her long hair is the color of dried grass – a pale sun-bleached brown. She is wearing an ankle-length dark skirt and a white blouse.

I study the other two paintings. The same figure is in both of them, blending almost imperceptibly into the washy background.

But I don't remember painting anyone. Only the scene outside.

In the second painting, she is running away from the house, her hair streaming behind her. In the third, the garden is awash in shades of dark blue, with a skim of moonlight outlining the trees and sparkling off the spray of water. The figure's white blouse shimmers in the darkness. She is standing perfectly still, looking toward the house, her face in darkness, her hair etched in moonlight. It's as if she's waiting for someone. But who?

My stomach twists into a tight knot of fear. I tear all three paintings into little bits with trembling fingers, push up the screen and shove the pieces through the narrow opening. I rest my chin on tight fists. As I watch the pieces spiral slowly down through the heavy air, I know this won't make the problem go away, but I feel better just for the action.

A swish of movement below catches my eye. The tail of the fat gray cat sways through the long grass toward a sparrow busily shaking water around itself in a lichen-streaked birdbath. Sunlight transforms the clear drops into rainbow jewels.

I pick up the nearest object — a slipper — reach out as far as I can and throw it. I just miss the cat. Startled, he flattens himself on the ground, ears rigid, tail still. The sparrow flutters away. At the same time, something bigger rises near the birdbath, behind the bushes, and runs toward the neighbor's yard. Purr forgets to be King of the Jungle and sits up to watch.

The hat, gray jacket and shoulder-length hair of the boy-statue from the cemetery disappear beneath the apple trees, but a few seconds later I catch a final glimpse before the figure ducks through the hedge that separates the two yards. Hallucinations don't run and hide, do they? They can't make leaves and branches move. Can they? I spot a small greenish-gray roof, barely visible amongst the trees close to the riverbank, not far from where the figure darted through the foliage.

I race down the two flights of stairs and out the back door, across the grass, under the apple trees and straight to the spot where the boy disappeared.

CHAPTER EIGHT

There is a clear gap in this hedge, similar to the one that leads into the cemetery on the other side of the garden. I cut through it and walk along the neighbor's hedge until I come to another green wall, six feet high, made of honeysuckle bushes and a deep tangle of heavy vines. I pace in front of the barrier trying to peer through the dense foliage.

Suddenly the sun highlights a small patch of white. I push aside the curtain of vines and find an old wooden gate with a curved trellis.

Behind it, a rough path leads through leggy bushes with flat canopies of green flames above. The smell is earthy and dense, the glint of the river just ahead.

I swing open the gate and follow the dirt path. It takes me a second or two to realize that behind another thick mass of vines I've found the small building with the gray roof. I press my hand against its cool stones. It's real, all right. Before I can change my mind I knock on the door, my heart pounding in my ears.

No one answers. The place is probably just full of tools and ancient garden furniture, but I try the latch anyway and to my surprise the door glides open. Inside, a greenish light comes from three small windows, the outside of their panes smothered in suckers and leaves. The corner of one pane is broken, and a reddish stem has trailed in and twisted itself up and over the low ceiling, its new leaves pale jade in the cool light.

I sense movement in the far corner, and when I turn to look, a door on the river side of the room slowly closes. I tiptoe across the floor and open it cautiously. Nothing moves in the dim grove of trees or bushes nearby. I close the door and walk slowly back across the room, not touching anything but looking around eagerly.

The small chamber is outfitted with everything a person would need. There's a miniature stone fireplace, with logs piled halfway up the wall beside it; on the other side is a single row of tattered books — *Below the Dark, The Intruder, Familiar Spirits* and other curious titles. The biggest one is called *The Encyclopedia of Psychic Science,* whatever that is. In front of these sits a sagging couch covered with pillows and faded quilts. In an open clothes rack near the front door hang two jackets, a half-dozen T-shirts, two plain white shirts and one pair of blue jeans.

Tucked in the corner by the back door is a two-burner stove and shelves of supplies. Most of the cans are vegetables — tomatoes, baked beans, corn, kidney beans, chick peas — with a couple of tins of milk near the back; the packages and cellophane bags are dried peas, cornmeal, flour, rice and Kraft Dinner. On a separate shelf are cardboard boxes of different colors. All teas. All herbal. Camomile, rose hip, chicory root, elderberry. A loaf of brown bread covered with a damp tea towel stands on the table beside a big chunk of yellow cheese, a teapot, one clean mug and plate, and a long bread-knife.

When I walk past the old couch I have the queasy feeling I'm being watched. But there's no one at the leafy windows, no one at the doors. *Get out of here. Go!* But as I move quickly across the hearth rug toward the door the air shifts like something alive. I know I'm in the same room, but now there's a fire in the grate. Flowered furniture with black metal arms and legs has replaced the spring-sagged couch. I wait, excited, tight inside. And then it comes.

"Nikos?" The name is repeated once. Twice.

I want to run, but the walls of the room lurch around me like an ancient merry-go-round. I grab the wooden mantel for support and close my eyes. When I open them everything is normal again. Normal? What's that? I put one foot in front of the other, barely feeling the floor – past the bookshelves, past the cold fireplace and out the door.

I find my way back to the hole in the hedge and across the garden toward Thea's house. Thunder rumbles and the orange sun disappears behind a black hand of cloud. As I reach the pond a sharp earthy stench rises, tightening my throat. I'm so shaky I'm not sure I can make it to the house.

In front of me is a stone seat with a wide back and arms. I sit down and try to catch my breath. Flashes of light pop in front of my eyes. I close them tightly and rub the lids with my fingertips.

When I open them again day has become night. A slender man with smooth black hair and a slice of a mustache over an arrogant mouth is standing right in front of me – shouting. The words are garbled at first, but they slowly become clear.

"… warned you, Susannah. Your father and I have … best interests at heart. You are to be *my* wife. The wedding is settled. You cannot live in some fantasy world with that – that foreign creature. He's nothing. I warned you. And now I've done it. I've fired him."

"You can't do that, Jeremy!" a girl's voice cries. "The owner of the house hired him. You're only renting. You have no right. He wouldn't leave me!"

The thin mouth laughs, but the eyes remain fierce. "I can do anything I wish. He's fired. Packed his bags."

"No! He wouldn't! You're lying. Like Papa. You're both liars!" The words are loud in my ears, and yet I don't know where they're coming from. From me?

The dark angular face leans closer. "He couldn't wait to get away. I told you! He's a pathetic weakling, as well as a brute."

"No. No! NO!" I look away from the dark intensity of his eyes. They're liars! Papa, Jeremy … both liars.

Cold wet splotches hit my face. Startled, I look up to see a thick oval of mist between me and the man. At the same time, there's a faint click in my head and a jab of pain that takes my breath away. A crack of thunder overhead lifts me off the stone seat, and I run full tilt through rain that stings my bare arms and legs.

Safely in the kitchen, I hang on to the edge of the table, head bent, heart pounding so hard it shakes my body. When a small voice pipes up from under my hands, I stagger back with a yelp.

"You said no go outside again. You said going to sleep. Fibber!"

How much does it take to make a mind snap?

"Aren't you supposed to be at day care or something?" I gasp at the tabletop.

"Wee knows way home. Thea need me. Be safe," the little voice continues. "Thea 'fraid of big storms."

"Thea not be safe anywhere right now. Thea losing her mind." I try hard to keep the fear out of my voice. "You're supposed to go to that Sunny Days place, aren't you? Before lunch?"

"Mrs. Horrible Dohlan drop me off. I wait. I hide. She go away. I come home."

"Everyone will be angry with you."

"Don't care. Thea need me."

"Well, come out from under there. I'll get Germaine to call Sunny Days and leave a message."

"No Sunny Days?" the little voice asks, hope in every word.

"No Sunny Days. It's a rainy day, anyway."

A chair is pushed aside.

"Germaine spank," she whispers, creeping from her hiding place.

"She won't spank anyone. You run up to my room. You can help me take down the paintings this afternoon. I'll talk to Germaine."

The smile Wee flashes me is pure joy and then she's gone. I let out a long shaky sigh. Some day this has been, and it's only – I glance at the kitchen clock – twelve-fifteen.

My mind whirls with questions. Who lives in the little cottage? Do the neighbors know they have a tenant in their garden? Is it the dark thin man with the mustache? No. Whoever lives there wears jeans and T-shirts, not heavy gray suits. Does the man live in the neighbor's big brick house?

I feel a wild surge of alarm and repulsion when I think about him. Who is he? Who was he shouting at? Not me. Another girl's voice answered him, and she knew his name. Jeremy. And he called her – I feel cold all over – Susannah. That name again. But why did he look straight at me, as if I was Susannah? What am I seeing? Who *are* these people? And why did that misty cloud appear again?

Strange people who appear and disappear, hallucinations, bodiless voices. That crack on the head did more than wipe out my memories.

Think. Think. The cottage really does exist. I'm sure of that. The clothes and food and everything in it are real. But who is the boy, the one I thought was a statue? Is he a member of the neighbor's family? Or is he the "foreign creature"? Does he have permission to be there? He sneaks around as if he's hiding. What does he want? Why didn't he stay to talk to me?

I jump a foot in the air when Germaine bangs into the kitchen, vacuum cleaner in hand, the hose coiled around her neck like a striped cobra. I stifle a crazy giggle. Germaine the Snake Woman.

"Want to share the joke?"

"Just something I was thinking about."

"Hmph." She stuffs the vacuum into a broom closet.

"Did you clean my room?"

"Of course not. You told me never to touch your room again. I took down those rags last year and you went berserk."

"But cleaning's your job, right?"

She narrows her eyes. "Fine. I'll do it tomorrow. But don't get all hysterical if I vacuum up a few things you don't want vacuumed up."

"I promise. Thanks."

She grunts and rattles around in the broom closet, trying to hang up the hose amid the clutter.

I take a deep breath and explain about Wee's escape from Sunny Days prison camp.

A few minutes later I climb the stairs, vacuum cleaner in hand. A deal is a deal: one clean bedroom for one phone call to Sunny Days. Germaine might have her uses after all, even if she does drive a hard bargain.

CHAPTER NINE

When the machine sucks up one of the long scarves trailing down the wall, I take them all down, dump the pile of pushpins into an empty jam jar and shake each strip of fabric out the window. The dust hangs thick in the heavy wet air. The first burst of rain has slowed and everything outside tip-taps with dripping water.

Wee shows me where the washer and drier are in the low cobwebby basement. I can't remember how to use the machines, but Wee seems to know all about it. When the washer starts churning away I strip off her clothes and throw them in, too. A few of the thinner fabrics from my room shred in the machine, but most survive the dousing and overload of soap.

There are packages of diapers piled on the floor, so I give Wee a quick change and she sits happily humming on top of the drier wrapped in a comforter dragged out of a bundle waiting to be washed. Purr, nosy as always, slips down and joins us.

Upstairs again I separate Wee's clothes and dress her. Then I fold the fabrics in readiness to put them away in the top of the wardrobe. My next job will be to take down these strange paintings of Thea's. Frozen to the spot, it dawns on me – if I *am* Thea, as everyone says I am, then it was *me* who painted them.

Wee, sitting cross-legged on the bed with Purr on her lap, says in a sad voice, "Thea sad? You no like your pretty room? Thea's Dream Room all going gone?"

"Is that what Thea, uh, what I called it?" I ask, trying to concentrate on what she is saying.

She waves her skinny arms. "I no like Dream Room now – ugly, ugly."

I look around. The upper walls are dirty, the ceiling spotted and dingy. She's right. It is ugly, and with the paintings down it will be even uglier.

"Will you help me put the fabrics back?" I ask.

"Oh, yes!" She claps her hands.

Half an hour later, Wee and I lie side by side on the bed looking up at them. Now that they're free of dirt, the fabrics look like streaks of rainbow light across the ceiling. The cat purrs like a tiny motor boat on the pale blue comforter. I begin to drift off. Wee watches me from between Purr's ears, blinking slowly, like a dainty owl.

"The owl and the pussycat went to sea," I murmur.

She leans close to me. "Thea remember! Our story! In a bee-you-tee-ful pea-green boat!" Her laughter is a happy gurgle.

A brightly colored book floats across my inner eye, but vanishes when a loud clap of thunder slams overhead. With a screech Wee throws herself on me. A rush of cold wind blows in the window. Purr leaps off the bed and disappears into the open closet.

Another explosion builds and then dies into a decaying rumble. Wee's bony grip strangles my arm.

"Is it *me* who's afraid of storms?" I ask, pushing her away gently.

She stares straight into my eyes. "Not Thea. *Wee* 'fraid. Wee big fibber."

I laugh, and the sky opens up and rain pours straight down like a single gray sheet. Thunder grumbles again, but seems to be on the other side of the river now. Wee buries her head in my arm and lets out a thin wail, but it's mostly acting. I pull the comforter up and over us in a light warm cocoon. She lets out a happy sigh, and I realize I am happy too. It comes as a shock. For this moment, *at* this moment, I am happy. The tight little face with its bright eyes smiles up at me. She snuggles closer.

"Love Thea. I do."

Well, one thing is clear. Wee is certain who I am — I'm Thea. I don't think anyone could get her to lie about that. Does it really matter if I remember this house with different furniture? So what if I remember a different garden? Maybe the thing to do is to start working on Thea's real-life memories. Thea, in her Dream Room, probably made up a girl named Susannah out of wishes and daydreams — a Susannah who lived here with different parents; with old-fashioned solid furniture that gleamed from beeswax and lemon oil; with a perfect flower garden and fat goldfish flashing through crystal-clear pond water. Thea's Dream Room. Thea's Dream Family. Thea's Dream Garden.

The warmth makes me drowsy. The rain slows to a steady rush. Do I hear a whisper? From above the bed? My eyes are heavy with sleep. I can hardly open them. Through the blur, a figure like a watery shadow, floats behind the scarves. Long hair spreads out in soft whirling patterns around its head. The face drifts down, presses against the fabric like a butterfly pushing through a thin cocoon.

"You didn't make me up," a voice whispers. "And I won't let you go. Not yet."

Two white arms break through the scarves and trail down toward me. I want to scream, but I can't breathe. I can't warn the little girl beside me. Something light touches my forehead and I slip feet first into blackness — like a stone dropping into a deep pool. From somewhere close by a man's voice calls out, "Forgive me ... forgive me ..."

CHAPTER TEN

I awake and sit straight up, startled and disoriented. A long bony face hangs over the carved foot of the bed, staring.

"Did you take down all the scarves on the ceiling?" it asks. "They've been rearranged. And everything is so, like ... *clean*."

"What are you doing here? And how long have you been standing over us like a ghoul?"

"A ghoul?" Ellie sneers. "What's a ghoul?"

"You are."

"You talk funny. Like a librarian or something. It's weird."

"Perhaps."

"Why did you take down those stupid curtainy things? You said they'd stay there until you left for good."

"What I do in this room is my own affair."

"'What I do in this room is my own affair,'" she mimics. "You used to lock me out. 'My room's off limits,' you'd say. All because I borrowed your stupid paints. Once! Just once! Now you don't even know if this *is* your room, do you? You don't remember it, do you? I don't know who the

68

heck you are." Her thin lips pinch into a pointy little smile. "And neither do you. Hah!"

"What do you mean, leave for good? Was Thea ... was I going to run away?"

"You were going to take off before Mama and Daddy left for England. Germaine said you'd never leave us kids. But you said you were going – and you almost always did what you said you were gonna do."

"Thea wouldn't leave Wee ... would she?"

"See? Even *you* talk about yourself as if you're someone else. I figure you might take Wee. But you'd leave me behind, wouldn't you?" For a second there's a flash of something in her eyes. Anger? Hurt?

How could I run away? Where would I go? But I don't say this to Ellie. Instead, I demand, "What exactly are you doing in my room if it's off limits?"

"Dinner's ready. Daddy says you need some stability, so he even got Mama to be home for dinner. She's not happy. She had to cancel a meeting, and you know what she's like when that happens."

"No, I don't."

"She gets cranky and orders people around – like, I always have to clean my room or show her my homework or something. And then she just glances at it really quick, and orders me to do something else. So get up, for cripes sake."

"We'll be right down." I point to the sleeping Wee. "No need to wait. And don't come in without knocking next time."

"Some day, when you finally do run away, *I'll* get this

room. And I'll be the boss. I'll take down your stupid scarves and your ugly paintings and I'll have flowered wallpaper. And I'll eat pizza in bed like you used to do. Hah!" She walks away, head high.

At the door, she glares at me down the length of her long nose. "I've decided that you're not Thea, so what you say doesn't matter. Thea didn't have that stupid spaced-out look on her face all the time. She wore lots of terrific-looking makeup, and even if she was crabby sometimes at least she made an *effort*. I can't see you making an *effort*. I don't like you. I don't know who you are, but I hope you take off soon."

"I'll leave when I'm good and ready," I say to her back. "And I probably won't bother to say goodbye."

The door slams behind her, but not before I see her startled expression. I don't like her, with her beady little eyes and her sneering mouth.

Wee's diaper stinks. I wake her up and take her to the bathroom, strip her down and stick her in warm shallow water. Under the tub, I find a bottle of shampoo. I dip her back in the water and wash her tangled hair. While she sits on the toilet and rubs her head with a thin towel, I scrub my face, trying to wash away the strange dream of the girl floating in shimmering scarves. Maybe the hallucinations are growing. I towel myself until my skin burns.

Downstairs Wee yanks on my T-shirt when I head toward the dining room.

"No, Thea," she whispers. "No eat here."

She's right. No dining-room furniture in the mahogany-lined room. Just a big U-shaped desk, computer and rows of bookshelves.

"Mama works here," she says. "Can't go in."

"Where does Wilton – your dad – work?"

"Ooniversity. And booky room. Down hall."

Papa's study. No. Stop. I have to suppress the other house. No more imaginary Papa. This clearly is not a dining room – not anymore – even if I am sure that daily meals were once eaten here on lace tablecloths and shiny green-edged dishes with gold-filigree flowers. And how could I know that the Papa of my imagination used the old study down the hall when I don't even remember that Wilton works there when he's home from the university? Susannah and this Papa person are not, and never were, real.

As I pull the dining-room door closed, a thin whisper drifts through the narrow space toward me.

"Remember me ..."

I slam the door shut, grab Wee's hand and march us to the kitchen.

Chapter Eleven

The kitchen table is spread with Chinese take-away. Agatha is pouring something labeled Perrier into a glass and complaining loudly.

"But they're missing. Surely you could have checked, Wilton. They did this the last time. We can't eat mushu pork without them."

"What's missing?" I ask.

Wee slides onto the chair beside me and leans against my shoulder. Will she ever stop clinging?

Agatha sighs. "Mushu are pancakes rolled around a filling. And Wang's Palace has forgotten the pancakes. Again. Wilton never checks the order. They always forget something at that place. Besides being my favorite dish, they're the only thing you'll eat."

Wilton looks crestfallen. "I am sorry, Thea."

I shrug. "Doesn't matter. I don't remember what I like. The rest smells delicious. But you don't dish the food right out of the containers, do you?"

Ellie snorts. "See, Mama? I told you she wasn't Thea."

"Don't be silly, Ellie." Agatha rubs her cheeks with the

palms of her hands. "I need a cigarette."

"But, Mommeee ..." Ellie moans. I stare at her. "Well, it *was* your idea to never use bowls, Thea. You said it made dishwashing easier."

I smile sweetly. "Makes sense. But I'm not Thea, remember? Pass the rice, please?"

Ellie looks both embarrassed and indignant.

Wee sits expectantly, waiting for me to spoon food onto her plate.

"Here." I hand her a carton of deep-fried pastry triangles. "You're old enough to do it yourself."

She looks hurt but does as she's told, only spilling a bit. "See? You can do it."

She brushes a few greasy crumbs off her shirt and offers me a flushed and pleased face.

"Now listen, Thea." Agatha's voice is still tightly wired. "I'm very upset about what happened today with Wee. Her teacher from Sunny Days called, absolutely furious. She told me that Mrs. Dohlan from Wee's morning day-care center dropped her off at Sunny Days at noon, but she ran home instead. Wee cannot just leave nursery school whenever she feels like it. Sunny Days may be close to home, but Wee must learn to stay there. And you can wipe that smile off your face. When they called Mrs. Dohlan at twelve-thirty, she had just heard from Germaine. The police could have been involved!"

I can't help it. I laugh out loud. "Took them long enough to figure out she'd disappeared. You might want to check them out more closely." I spear a piece of chicken with my fork. "Besides, I didn't ask her to run away from the place."

Wilton gives a dry little cough as if about to speak. Agatha glares at him.

"We do know that, Thea," she continues. "And there is no need for sarcasm. You should have sent her right back. You're the one who kept harping about how she was too dependent on you. You were the one who asked us to try Sunny Days. You thought Mrs. Dohlan was neglecting the older children and slowing Wee's progress. And now you encourage the child to stay home all afternoon. There's a long waiting list at Sunny Days – children who don't regress into diapers at the least provocation."

"And who's fault is that? Thea's no doubt. I have a feeling that no matter what happens it's always Thea's fault. Even Ellie's rotten behavior is Thea's ... my fault."

Ellie looks alarmed.

Agatha doesn't shift from her purpose. "Sunny Days took Wee as a special student, but they'll drop her if we're not careful, and then where will we be! You must be more careful –"

"I didn't know where to take her back *to*. Besides, the storm was coming. What's the big deal? Germaine phoned. Wee can try again tomorrow. Just show me where it is and I'll walk her there myself."

"Maybe Thea's right," Wilton offers. "She really knows Wee best."

I want to shout into his gentle silly face, *Don't you get it yet? I don't know her at all*. But I keep quiet. The kid's face is already crumpled with worry.

Agatha picks at the cuff of her sweater. "I hope that isn't a criticism of me, Wilton."

"Of course it isn't, Aggie," he says fondly, "but we promised the doctor we would try ... Remember?"

"Yes. Yes, of course. Being harsh is so counter-productive." She adds in a stilted tone, "Perhaps you'd like to tell Thea about tomorrow's plan?"

Wilton nods. "Oh, right. Uh, well, Thea, Germaine left a note that Dr. Browning's office called with a reminder about your appointment tomorrow afternoon at two. We'll have to order a taxi. You didn't tell us you had an appointment, you see, and both Aggie and I have other commitments. You, er, understand, of course ... yes?"

I stare at the food on my plate. Why did I cover everything in this horrible sticky pink sauce?

"Unless ... unless you feel you really must have one of us along," he says, and I look up just in time to catch the warning glance Agatha sends him.

"Just leave instructions for the driver," I say coldly. "I'll go on my own. I prefer it."

Wilton coughs again, but Agatha keeps right on going. "You must see that this accident of yours has been a terrible strain on all of us. Your father and I are so far behind in our work we're frantic. All this drudgery at home, as well. It's been a nightmare. As for tomorrow, I'll have to get groceries after my sessions. Everything has been so neglected."

"Of course. I understand." I slide my fork through the

congealing sauce. "I've only been here one day and already I understand. You and Wilton come first — kids come somewhere after grocery shopping. Right?"

Ellie chokes on a mouthful of food. Her eyes have a strange guarded look.

In a sorrowful voice Wilton says, "That was very hurtful. I'm surprised at you, Thea."

Agatha butts in. "Well, I'm not. She can't possibly know how hard it's been for you, Wilton. Or for me. How could she know? As she said, she's only been home for one day."

I snort. "It's been hard: On you and Wilton?"

"You know very well what I mean. It's been hard on everyone. In this family we work *together*, not against one another. If it's going to work, you'll have to fit in as soon as possible and pull your own —"

"Oh, please, don't say it!"

Pale freckles stand out on her cheekbones. "I'm warning you, Thea. I don't want you starting that old nonsense again."

"What nonsense?"

Someone nudges my leg. Ellie's little eyes are glittering. With a warning? For me?

Agatha carries on. "The defiance. The storytelling. The sulking. The bad temper. You used to be so … biddable. Then these past few months — before the accident — you became difficult …"

"She doesn't remember, Agatha," Wilton says softly.

"Maybe. Or maybe Germaine is right. Maybe Thea remembers everything and is doing all this out of spite."

Her bottom lip trembles. "She's certainly behaving the same as she was just before — the hospital."

My hands squeeze into fists. "Don't you get it yet? I don't know who this Thea is you're talking about. I don't know who I am! I don't know *you*. And from what I've seen so far, I don't want to!"

With that, I grind back my chair and march straight down the hall and out the front door.

Chapter Twelve

I stand at the edge of the walk. I don't want to turn left toward the gloomy cemetery. To my right, under the shiny green arch of elm trees, the sidewalk slides alongside a narrow boulevard, then swings sharply and disappears behind a distant hedge.

Somewhere nearby, a door slams. I move quickly to the right. The cracked sidewalk is littered with small twigs and uncurled leaf buds. The gray clouds have thinned and a watery sun casts twisted ribbons of pale light through the puddles. I run through them, kicking water up my legs. When I look back I can't see anyone at the Dreadful Crew's gate, so I slow to a walk. My head thumps painfully. If I'd stayed in that kitchen it might have exploded all over their dinner.

At the end of the street I look toward the busy main road to my left, where traffic swishes by in a hazy fog. Where can I go? From behind the neighbor's sprawling brick house, a wheelbarrow, piled high with glistening weeds, heads up the long driveway, followed by a pair of jean-clad legs and heavy work boots. The boy from the cemetery is attached to those solid boots. No imaginary being here. His long caramel-colored hair has been tied in a ponytail, and the funny flat-topped hat is pulled low over his forehead.

Should I go over and confront him?

I hesitate too long. A gabble of voices grows behind me. Arms wrap around my legs. I sigh with frustration and relief. Wee has made the decision for me.

Ellie bears down on us. "You're not supposed to run off unless someone is with you, you stupid little kid!" she shouts.

Wee whines into my leg, "Thea need me. She sad."

Ellie pokes her in the back. Wee wriggles under it, crying pitifully.

"Cut it out, Ellie!" I snap.

"Well, she's not supposed to. It's all your fault anyway. You better come home. Or else."

"Or else what?"

"Yes, you come home," Wee begs, tugging my hand.

"When I'm good and ready."

The now empty wheelbarrow and the boy have disappeared behind the house. He never once looked in my direction, but I'm certain he saw me.

"Honestly, Thea," Ellie sneers, "you've ruined everyone's dinner. Just like always. Daddy's locked away in his room and Mama's going out after all." I decide that Ellie is a mixture of dark gray, acid green and red-brown. Bitter, nasty and something else – that secret anger or hurt I saw earlier in my room.

"I thought dinner was ruined because Wilton didn't check for the pancakes," I say. "And besides, I'm not Thea, remember?"

"Don't be stupid," she says, her lip curled.

"One day your face will stay that way." A sour-faced nurse said that to me one day when I'd refused to let her take a third blood sample in an hour.

"You *have* to come home!" Ellie wails, stamping a sandaled foot in a puddle. "I'm not doing dishes alone anymore. Wee breaks too many and you're the oldest. It's not fair. And my face will *not* stay this way." Her bottom lip quivers and she looks like a skinny version of her mother.

Wee tugs again. "Come now, Thea. Ellie allas yells. You no yell."

"Just a second, Wee," I say, then I ask Ellie, "Do you know who lives next door?" I point at the brick house. "Is their name Nikos?"

"Their name is Whitehead," Ellie says in a sulky voice. "They've gone to France for six weeks. They're really old. Who cares about them!"

"So no one lives there now?"

"No. Come on, let's go."

"A boy live there," says Wee.

Ellie folds her arms. "He doesn't count. Germaine says he just showed up one day on the Whiteheads' doorstep, and they hired him to mind the yard and house. Germaine says the Whiteheads are too trusting. He'll rob them blind, she says."

Wee pulls on my shirt. "He can fly."

"What?" I stare at her.

"He can't fly, you little twerp." Ellie rolls her eyes.

"What's his name?" I ask.

"I know," Wee says proudly. "And he does, too, fly!"

"He does not!" Ellie jeers. "He just sits in their trees sometimes and looks around. He's weird."

I turn to Wee. "You know his name?"

"It be Fitz ... Fitz ..." She frowns.

Ellie pushes in. "Germaine told Mama it's Lucas Fitzgerald."

Fitzgerald? A piercing hiss and then a sharp pain slides into my head. I know that someone is here with me. Someone who isn't me. Together we drift softly, softly, sinking through wet concrete, through leaves and roots, and the earth closes over our heads and sucks us down, down into utter stillness.

CHAPTER THIRTEEN

"You can't faint like that and expect to get up this morning," Wilton says, tapping his fingertips on my bedstead. "Stay here until it's time to go see Dr. Browning. And don't forget to tell him about your fainting spell."

"I promised Wee I'd take her to nursery school."

"We'll, uh, arrange something," he says.

Agatha chews on her thumbnail. Her wiry hair has been dragged into a fuzzy ponytail. The skin is tight over her sharp nose, but the pouches under her eyes are soft with heavy wrinkles. She looks tired and ill. "You scared us silly. Our doctor was very good to come out last night."

"But isn't that his job?" I ask.

"Doctors rarely come to people's homes anymore, Thea."

I'm sure she's wrong. Didn't Dr. Johanson come to see Papa only last month when he had one of his terrible headaches? Those ridiculous terrifying headaches when he ties his dressing-gown belt around his head to ease the pain, staring into a dark world I can't see, where he says evil things lie coiled and pulsing, waiting for him.

I swallow hard. I'm doing it again. Remembering this

Papa person from Thea's pretend family.

Why would I make up someone in such torment?

Then I remember something that did happen – the evening before. Just before I fainted I was certain that someone had entered my head, someone other than Thea. Isn't that what crazy people think? That someone else, other voices, are inside their heads? What would you say to that, Dr. Browning? I don't intend to find out.

"Are you okay, Thea?"

I can hear Wilton's voice, but his face has become blurred behind a gauzy light that hangs between us. Oh no, not again! Fear clutches my stomach, but I can't look away. In front of Wilton's head a face is slowly forming, round and thick-fleshed with staring blue eyes and thin white hair standing straight out from the scalp.

Papa. He looks past me with terrified eyes, as if he, too, sees something he can't bear to look at, yet can't look away from.

"No! Not him!" a voice whispers nearby. "He can't make us change our minds. Not now. It's too late. Tell him it's too late!"

"It's too late," I say out loud.

"Thea? Are you okay?" Wilton asks, and to my relief the old man's face dissolves like melting wax.

Wilton tries to smile but fails. "Stay in bed until you go to the doctor, okay? Germaine has agreed to drive you to the clinic. We want someone with you in case you take another turn. And the way you look right now ..."

Agatha nods. "And let's forget about anything said at supper last night. I ... we were all tired. And now we must get Wee to day care and ourselves to work." One of her swollen fingers touches my hand. "You'll be okay?"

I pull away and nod.

"Thea, come on now."

"I don't feel well," I say in a low tone.

"About last night —"

"Like you said, forget it."

"It's this pregnancy and the accident, Thea. The worry, you know? Everything's in turmoil. We'll dialogue later tonight, okay?"

Dialogue? Yeah, sure. I close my eyes and roll away from them.

When the door closes I can still hear them talking. I ease out of bed and creep close to the paneled wood.

"Maybe one of us should go to Dr. Browning with her," Wilton says.

"Go ahead if you like. I can't miss any more time. Those visits to the hospital added up."

"Look, aren't you worried about her, Aggie?"

"Of course I am. That blank-stare posture she goes into — I can't tell if she's faking it. You know how dramatic she always was. Moping around here like Cinderella in ashes. She's a very good actor. This could go on for a long time. I'm worried sick!"

"Then one of us *should* go with her," Wilton replies.

"How about this. I'll leave a message on Browning's

answering machine that if he has any worries about Thea he's to call us. I don't think he will. After all, he'll want to keep her trust, not blab to us. She looks better today. Last night the GP said she'd just overdone it yesterday. She's physically fine, Wilton, but her mental state ..." Their voices fade down the hall.

I crawl back under the covers and lie very still. They really don't care what happens to me. Oh, maybe there's a bit of guilt or worry, but it's all tied in to how my accident has affected them. How on earth did Thea stand living here?

I push The Parents into a cupboard in the back of my mind and try to sleep, but like a pale moon, the wavery picture of the white-haired man slides up behind my closed eyelids. The darkness that dropped over me last night hovers behind him like a black cloak, and I feel myself sinking into it. A voice, clear and intense, whispers, "Fitzgerald." My eyes snap open, my heart pounding.

Why does the name Fitzgerald frighten me so? It's the boy's name. Maybe I've already met the boy – when I was the other Thea. I'd have forgotten him like I've forgotten everyone else. But why react to his name by fainting? And if I knew him before the accident, why hasn't he spoken to me? Why skulk around? My head buzzes with questions. I sit up and gaze out the window. It's sunny and the early-morning warmth steams hazily across the garden.

There's even a haze in here. I blink hard. A thin ripple of light shimmers in front of the window, and another face forms in the air and floats toward me. It's not the sagging face of the old man; the features are darker and younger. Not a handsome face but warm and open, with a flop of black curly hair above a broad forehead, heavy-lidded deep-set eyes and a wide full mouth. The mouth is moving. He's speaking but I can't hear him. I sit up and he draws back from me, his expression one of sadness, of pleading.

I don't know this face, yet I want to hold its image in my mind, memorize it, store it away, touch it. My throat tightens with sorrow for something precious that is lost, and something else – something I once experienced, sweet and dangerous and unwavering. As I gaze at this face I know that someone, me – or *her*, the other one, who whispers inside me – loved this person once, loved him in a way she had never loved anyone else.

My throat pulses with blood, heavy and thick. Slowly, despite my wish to keep him here, he, too, disappears. I swallow a choking sob. What's happening to me?

Four faces float through the empty rooms of my brain, merging, then drifting apart again: Papa, with his thick jowls and pale eyes, the thin dark face of the man by the pond, the narrow brown face of the boy from the garden. And finally, the open tender gaze of those liquid eyes under glistening black curls. But hovering nearby, always, is the whispering girl named Susannah, who flits in and out of my head and won't let me see her, except in washy paintings, in one fleeting reflection on a windowpane, in the pale floating scarves above my bed.

What do these fantasy people want with me?

I can't take this. I throw back the covers and struggle to my feet. I'll focus on other things. Concentrate. On the sunlight that streams through the window, on the dust I forgot to wipe from the window ledge, on the tight fists my hands have become.

"Go outside. Get out of here. Get out." My voice is harsh in the still, warm air.

Should I take a box of colored chalks and some paper? No, I can't. What if the girl shows up again in the next drawing?

At the back of the wardrobe I find a dark green sundress. It's too long, but loose and cool. I slip on a pair of sandals. The room is growing hot and humid, so I open the window wide. A stray breeze stirs the rainbow fabrics and carries the sweet scent of blossoms from the garden below.

In the kitchen, Germaine, a cigarette between yellowed fingers, grunts and pushes cold toast at me.

"Here. Don't want to waste good food. Put marmalade on it. And eat some cheese. Protein. Don't want you fainting again. You're not supposed to be up, are you?"

Surprised at her concern, I say, "Thanks, I'm okay," around a mouthful of bittersweet orange.

"If you get sick again I don't get my regular hours back, do I?"

I should have known.

"I hear they roped you into taking me to the shrink's."

"Somebody has to, and I knew those parents of yours wouldn't. Just be ready on time. Two o'clock sharp."

"Germaine? Can I ask you something?"

"What?" Her forehead knots into a frown.

"Did Thea ... did I ever have friends over? I mean, before the accident? No one's called. Didn't I have a girlfriend ... or a boy I knew?"

She shakes her head. "You brought a girl or two home now and again, but you said they didn't like having to look after your sisters with you."

"So I always had to come home right after school?"

She nods. "To get supper. It's a wonder you kids don't have malnutrition. I make stews and stuff sometimes, but I'm not hired to cook. I do breakfasts now 'cause I'm paid extra."

"Can I ask you something else?"

"I guess." But she doesn't look very happy about it.

"It's nothing personal. I just wondered if you knew if anybody named Fitzgerald used to live around here."

"Isn't the hired kid next door named Fitzgerald?"

"I think so. But I have a feeling there were more living there once. I don't know why."

"What kind of crazy notion do you have in your head now?"

"I'm just asking."

"Look, the kid appeared one day looking for a job. And the Whiteheads, not the smartest people on the block, hired him, no questions asked. He's staying in the little house by the river. Why're you asking?"

"I just saw him and wondered."

"Well, keep away from him. He's a weird one."

"Weird?"

"Yeah. I tried to talk to him once, but he looked right through me. Didn't say a word. Gave me the creeps. He'll be gone at the end of July. You've got enough loopy things going on in that head without hanging out with some other kook. I was going to suggest your parents hire him to mow the lawn, but I didn't know if the kid would understand me. Or whether you'd all end up murdered in your beds."

"The Whiteheads' yard looks nice." I remember neat lawns and tidy flower beds. "Maybe he's not too weird. And why do you always talk about Thea – me – as if *I* was … strange, even before the accident?"

"You wanna know what you were like? A head full of nonsense most of the time. Dreamy-faced. Making things up. I hoped that hit on the head would knock some sense into you. But it doesn't look like it." She squints at me suspiciously through dense blue smoke.

"Did she – I mean, did I really make things up?"

Germaine laughs, a short sharp bark. "Are you kidding? You lived in a fantasy world. Talking your head off one minute and silent Sam the next, with a butter-wouldn't-melt face. When you weren't mooning about you were snarking at those parents of yours – not that I blamed you, mind. Worried yourself sick about the little one. Fought like cats with the other one more and more lately."

"You didn't like Thea, did you?"

"I never said that." She grinds her cigarette out in a nearby saucer. "You did your thing and I did mine. That's all."

I wave my cup of tea in front of her. "I'll take this

outside, okay? I'll wash it later."

I leave her lighting up another cigarette and avoiding my eyes. The screen door clacks shut behind me. As I walk across the grass, Purr bounds out of the undergrowth and winds his long smoky tail around my bare legs. My feet and sandals are wet, but the air is warm, the sun strong. Despite feeling so dragged out and sick this morning, I feel calm – and stronger – walking in this peaceful place.

I wander around the edges of what must have once been flower beds. Purple irises poke their bearded faces out of the tangled undergrowth, last year's hollow weed stems and seed pods rising high above them. Petals from the trees flitter past like pale moth wings.

I pull at a handful of stiff brown stems. They come up easily. Lower down, new thistles grow juicy and fat. They prickle my hands, but I don't mind. It keeps my head focused. Their roots are deep and hard to pull. Other weeds, chickweed and ground ivy, grip the soil with millions of tiny fingers along their trailing suckers.

A new energy gives me the strength to pull. And pull. Little balls of soil and decaying leaves scatter everywhere. The formal garden, the one in the paintings – the one in my dreams – is here somewhere, hidden away like secret treasure. I can find it. I *have* to find it. Purr sits beside me, watching. Before long I'm straining into the middle of the flower bed, dragging out anything that looks even remotely like a weed.

Aha! There's a patch of baby's breath, with buds like tiny

pearls, and farther along a little cluster of bleeding hearts, their crystal flowers bursting in two, a sticky tear on the end of each stamen. The pile of unearthed weeds grows higher. My fingers burn. Soon my knees are deep in mud, sandals cast to one side, skirt tucked up.

The sun grows hotter. My head starts to throb. I sit back on my heels and push damp bangs off my forehead with a sweaty forearm. The flower bed suddenly looks very very long, and I've barely made a dent in the weeds. But at least little patches of color gleam against the black soil of the small square right in front of me and this gives me hope.

Purr, who's been chasing shiny beetles and prickly little wormlike creatures through the moist earth, looks intently at the broad blossoms of the neighbor's apple tree, which hangs over the hedge above me.

"If that's another poor defenseless bird you're gawking at, forget it," I say. "I'm not going to let you commit birdicide."

He remains rigid and unblinking. I shade my eyes with one muddy hand and ease to a standing position, trying to locate the thing that interests the Demon Cat. Two human eyes stare back at me from behind the blossoms. With a cry I fall back, landing on the weed pile.

The eyes evaporate. The branches sway wildly and a snowfall of petals cascades to the black soil at my feet.

I hear a soft thump on the other side of the hedge. The stupid idiot's fallen out of the tree! I scramble to my feet and take off running. Yes!

He won't escape this time.

Chapter Fourteen

I run to the gap in the hedge, bare feet churning up grass and mud. The sharp branches grab at my dress as I pass through the narrow space, but I keep right on going.

The boy is sitting under the tree rubbing an elbow. I am as silent as the cat, creeping along the shadow of the hedge until I step on a thistle and let out a tiny yelp. In a split second he's up and off.

"Wait!" I shout, clawing at the burning pain in my instep.

He breaks stride, hesitates, then continues, ponytail streaming out behind him.

"Damn you! Wait up!"

I limp to the tall barrier of green at the end of the yard and grope around until I find the white gate.

"Don't run away, please!" I cry, but my shout comes out as a gargle of pain.

I lean against the wall of the little house and pull the thorny needle out of my instep, then edge along the cool stone wall, push aside thick damp vines and rub at a grimy window.

Through the murky glass I can see the boy sitting cross-legged on the floor, his back against the old couch, his knees drawn up, his face toward the cold fireplace. Slowly he turns his head and we stare at each other for what seems like hours. Then he looks away, dismisses me.

All my anger at being spied on disintegrates. Now I'm the spy. I turn to go, embarrassed and fiery-cheeked.

The door clicks open and he stands on the threshold — slight, not much taller than me, wearing a green shirt and jeans. He moves to one side and I step into the room.

The bottom of my dress is wet, my feet muddy and sore. I shiver. The room is cold, despite the heat outside. The boy looks at my face, studying it carefully. Uncomfortable, I turn my back and perch on the edge of the couch.

What am I doing here?

He lights a small bundle of paper and kindling in the tiny fireplace. Then he goes into the kitchen, fills a tin washbasin with water from a puffing kettle, and sets the basin on the floor in front of me with a bar of soap and a rough towel. I put both feet in the warm water and can't hold back a sigh of pleasure. He puts the kettle back, returns and sits on a chair across from me, watching intently.

"Can you speak?" I ask finally.

He hesitates, then shrugs.

"Can you hear? Are you deaf?"

He shakes his head, and a secret smile curls the narrow lips. He has a very young, almost elfin face and a thin nose. The slanting eyes are full of strange and hidden things, and there is a curious stillness in their green darkness.

The kettle starts to blow a slow lazy whistle on the burner.

The boy gets up again and assembles cups and spoons. I dry my feet and legs, then lean back against the couch pillows. The fire grows higher, sending off small waves of fragrant heat. The light fabric of my dress steams gently. The room is so peaceful my muscles relax and I realize how tightly I've been guarding myself the past few days – as if waiting for something to explode behind me. Or in my head. I sigh and close my eyes.

Before I can drift lazily away, I see behind my eyelids a vision of this same room with that other, distant fire scattering around the darkened walls. Suddenly a face leans over mine. I try to open my eyes but can't. The face has no features and the hair is ringed in light. I'm in a dream, struggling to wake up, yet waiting, waiting for ... Something clatters behind me and I sit up, tense, ready for flight, eyes wide. The boy appears carrying a tin tray with two thick white cups on it.

I laugh nervously. "I – I almost fell asleep. I dreamed ... It's so comfortable here. Nice ..." My cheeks are hot.

I reach out and take one of the cups, pretending not to notice that my hand is shaking. I sip cautiously and try to keep from spilling. It tastes wonderful, not sweet but creamy and thick, with a chocolatey coffee flavor. The boy again sits cross-legged on the floor. His eyes never leave my face.

I study the bubbles that slide along the inside of my cup. For someone so shy, he certainly stares a lot.

"Why did you run away from me in the cemetery?" I ask quietly. "And then again today?"

He smiles, but those secret green eyes are still wary, guarded.

"Wee — the little girl, my smallest sister — she says you can fly," I say.

He laughs then, little hisses through his teeth.

I lean forward. "Look, can't you talk at all? It's hard holding a one-sided conversation."

He shrugs again.

"Could you talk if you wanted to?" I ask. "Just say yes or no, okay?"

He opens his mouth and in a surprisingly deep voice says, "Yes."

I feel a flutter along the skin on my arms, as if I've just seen something rare — a golden butterfly or exotic bird.

"But you don't talk to just anyone."

"No."

"You'd get along with Wee. She only uses the important words in a sentence. She's a bit, you know, slow ..." I stop, and then babble, "Not that I think you're like that — or that there's anything wrong if you are. I mean ... I'm sorry. It's just that ... oh heck." I stare uncomfortably at my clean bare toes.

The silence becomes thick and heavy. I look up, ready to apologize again, but he's staring over my shoulder.

The hair on the back of my neck stirs as if a hand has brushed lightly against it.

"What is it? What are you seeing?"

"Nothing. Light. Just misty light. It's gone now."

I hold the cup with both hands to stop the liquid from sloshing. I hear breathing behind me — as if someone is trying to catch their breath.

My next words come out in a husky croak. "Do you see anything now? Anything at all?"

"No."

"You don't talk much, but you can tell lies like anyone else, can't you?"

In one movement he's up and walking quickly toward the back door.

I scramble to my feet. "Look, I'm sorry, but I know you were seeing something. Purr, my cat, he sees it, too. Can't you — ?"

The door bangs shut behind him. When I fling it open he's striding through a grove of trees down the sloping bank toward the river, his back stiff, his whole manner telling me to stay away.

"Wait!" I call.

He drops out of sight.

"Fine! Play hide-and-seek. But I'm not coming back here again looking for you. And don't bother hanging around me anymore unless you've got something to say that matters!"

I slam the door, shocked by the echoes of my screeching voice.

"Good going, Thea, or whoever you are!" I mutter. "Your first possible friend in your new life and it takes you less than half an hour to drive him out of his own house."

CHAPTER FIFTEEN

When I pass a little orchard of stunted apple trees at the bottom of the Chalmers-Goodall yard, I spot a small storage shed nearly hidden by sprawling bushes. The tiny building has a lean-to attached, both sections roofed with wooden shingles. The door of the shed hangs on one hinge. Inside the small space are tangled badminton nets, wooden plant stakes, and rusting tins with faded insects and flowers on their labels.

The lean-to holds a few ancient gardening tools, including a long-handled shovel, a pitchfork and a wheelbarrow with a big rust-eaten wheel and high wooden sides. It squeals as I push it toward the small patch of cleared garden. With great concentration I load up my pile of weeds.

I stop now and again to see if the boy is nearby, but I can't spot him. Is his name Lucas, like Ellie said?

"Hey! Where have you been, missy!"

Germaine minces across the lawn in high heels.

I shade my eyes. "Why?"

"It's two o'clock. I've been looking everywhere for you. The doctor? Remember?"

She's wearing a tight orange dress and a fuzzy red cardigan. She shakes car keys at me. "Well? Those two won't like this – your being late."

"I'm not going."

"Not going?"

"Yes. I mean no – I'm not going."

"You're going, kiddo."

I stick out my chin. "I don't need a shrink. I can't remember things, that's all. Dr. Browning said it would all come back. I won't go just to hear him tell me the very same thing again."

She narrows her eyes and to my surprise says, "Yeah, well, I can't say I blame you. I don't hold with some of these psycho doctors. Do more harm than good, some do. But you might've warned me. I went home and changed."

"You look very nice."

She smoothes her skirt. "Well, no point in wasting the effort, is there? I'll go down to the corner market and get some early green beans. Then I might stop off at bingo before I head home."

"That's a good idea. Take some time for yourself."

"Now don't you come on to me like Miss Hoity-toity. I don't need your approval for anything."

"I'm sorry." I try to look sorry.

"Yeah, well … never mind."

"Before you go, could you phone the doctor's office and tell them I'm not coming? If *I* call them, they'll check with Wilton and Agatha."

"Butter me up with apologies so I'll do your dirty work, eh?"

"Please?"

"Okay. But you keep your trap shut about my time off. That's the deal." She turns to go.

"Germaine?"

"Yeah?"

"Thanks."

The side of her mouth twitches. "Let's just hope they don't hear about it, that's all. See you later. Don't forget the kids get home at four today. Ellie's picking up the little one at the nursery school. Sunny Days! Humph!"

With that, she minces her way back along the grass. I think we've come to a temporary truce, Germaine and I.

When I return to the house, I realize it's the first time I've been alone in it since I arrived. I walk slowly through the downstairs rooms. I have no idea what I'm looking for, but when I reach "Papa's study" I hesitate, then slowly turn the handle.

The room is still and silent. I sit down on a leather armchair facing the window with its upper rectangle of stained glass. Sunlight falls in patterned colors across the light blue rug. An oak desk stands with its back toward the window. I know that desk. It has three drawers down one side and two larger ones on the other. There's a small ink stain inside the shallow middle drawer. It's where Papa kept the household keys.

But who is remembering those keys? Thea? Susannah?

Shouldn't I feel something other than this passive distant curiosity, as if I'm looking at everything through the wrong end of binoculars?

I don't like this floating uneasy sensation. As I stand up an icy breeze swirls around my bare ankles. One of the papers on the desk lifts and ruffles lightly, as if a hand is moving it. And just behind me there is a breathy sound, faint but clear.

Someone is in the room with me.

Out of the corner of my eye I see a dark figure, still and watchful. When I whirl around a trembling laugh bubbles into my throat, for it's only a large sepia photograph on the wall, the head and shoulders of a man in a black suit with a high white collar.

But my laughter quickly dissolves when I recognize the round flaccid face with its large arched nose and small mouth. Papa stares at me with eyes that gleam with an eerie intensity. The eyes are cold and pale under heavy creased lids, assessing me with faint disgust. On the small brass plate attached to the frame is a name.

Samuel Billings Lever.

Scattered sounds form into whispers and then into louder voices all around me.

"Why, Papa? Why?"

"Because I say so, child. Because I won't have you degraded by associating with some papist foreigner! You are promised. To a fine man. There is no more to discuss."

"Papa, I simply won't be dismissed like this!"

The black-coated figure tears away from the photo and glides toward me. I can see the picture frame through his body, yet the face and eyes are solid – and blazing with fury, the thin lips working, spittle foaming.

"I am your father and you will obey me."

"I'm old enough now, Papa, to make my own decisions. I love him. I want to share my life –"

"Share your life? What *life* will you have with him? He'll destroy you. He'll take you away. You have obligations to the parish. To me." His face changes, becoming glazed with fear. "If you go, the parishioners will find out ... The diocese will realize that I ..."

The girl's voice softens. "Papa, I have begged you to retire. The church will understand. The stress, the constant visiting ... they'll understand. You won't have to tell them – about the headaches or the other thing –"

"You want me to retire, to go back east so you can slink off with that ignorant boor and breed like all the poor miserable women I see farther along the river –"

"Is that what you really believe, Father? That I'll change? That I'll become incompetent and stupid? You don't know him. He trained for different work in Greece. He's highly skilled. He's learning English quickly and we'll –"

"You will be ruined. And then I *will* have to retire, because of the humiliation. I've spoiled you, and now you've come to this – spiteful child. Punishing me for letting you be idle and foolish."

"Idle and foolish? Papa! I run this entire rectory with one

fourteen-year-old maid. I oversee all your arrangements, prepare food for meetings, do the laundry, the cooking. I do the church accounting, as Mr. McGifford is utterly hopeless at it. I do all the —"

Papa's face deepens to an angry red and his jowls quiver. "Enough! Your responsibilities are not so onerous that you can't find time for daydreaming about in that garden of yours. And look where *it* has got you — involved with a foreigner, a laborer —"

"I love him. If you had agreed that we could live here, I would have continued to fulfill my obligations to you. But you've made it clear we cannot stay. Therefore I am compelled to leave."

The words come from my mouth, yet the voice isn't mine.

The old man's anger once again subsides, and in its place the heavy features form themselves into an expression of maudlin pleading. "Susannah, don't go. Try and be reasonable, eh? Stay. Let me explain. Susannah, stay —"

"No! I have listened enough!"

A gauzy shape drifts away from me and hovers by the door, where for one brief second it becomes the figure of a tall girl dressed in a simple skirt and blouse, her hair wound into a heavy coil at the nape of her neck. As the door swings open she turns and looks straight at me.

I run after her, but the hall is empty. The door slams behind me with a crash. I fly up the stairs to the third floor, fling myself onto the bed and drag the comforter over my head. Despite the warm darkness, my teeth chatter.

If it's true that crazy people have visions and believe that someone else is taking over their heads sometimes, then I must be crazy — because now I have photographs coming to life right in front of me, and I'm hearing voices more and more, and the girl — she looked at me!

I sit up. No! No more voices. No more people appearing and vanishing. Not if I can help it. I'll fight it — with willpower. I'll concentrate hard on fighting it. I won't let images or sounds come into my head anymore — no lunatic Papas in book-lined studies, no dark-haired men yelling at me in the garden, no curly-haired men with soft eyes appearing like romantic fantasies in front of my eyes. It's pathetic. Really pathetic. With my luck the boy isn't real either — just another walking talking mirage.

Yes. I'll close them all off. And I'll shut down my mind to that imaginary girl — Susannah. I'll think about the garden. Hard work will chase away these intruders. It'll take days to clear away the weeds in just one flower bed, but I'll do it. I'll get rid of that choking mess, and then the deep-rooted perennials will come up again. Big fat peonies, long slender day lilies, startled black-eyed Susans, blue Canterbury bells, gangly hollyhocks. And order and peace will come with them.

Something like surprise flickers in the back of my mind. I know the names of specific flowers. Could *Thea* be remembering them — not Susannah? Maybe this is a sign that soon I'll remember Thea, too.

I fall asleep in a swirl of petals — broad pink and cream, pointed red and spotted orange, scattered blue and thick purple velvet. And green — light green, acid green, green as black as night and green the color of cotton shirts and dark slanted eyes ...

I wake up to the choking smell of wet soil and crushed weeds, my lungs bursting. I untangle myself from the cover and stagger to my feet. I can't ... can't breathe. I clutch the edge of the dresser and with all my strength and concentration suck air into my lungs. Spots of light jiggle in front of my eyes.

The big dresser's mirror is right in front of me. Dark smudges ring my eyes, and the skin on my cheeks and forehead is the color of watercolor paper. I gasp hot humid air into my chest. I've lost the bandage on my head. How? When?

I stare at the image until the whites around the dark irises grow larger. It isn't Thea in that mirror. It's someone else — a wide-eyed girl dressed in a dark green skirt and a fine white blouse with pale green ribbons at the neck. Long hair, parted above the wide smooth forehead, flows in thick shiny ropes over her shoulders. The face is narrow, oval — a beautiful face, even in its anger — with a slender nose, a trembling mouth and a strong rounded chin. The eyebrows are thick and arched above the vivid gaze.

She speaks to her image in the mirror. "What made you think you would *ever* be allowed to escape? Standing up to him didn't make any difference. It's all past. It's all too late. Just a repeat of all that's gone before. Even now you remain a prisoner. What a fool! What a stupid pathetic fool you are! The girl is no use to you. How can you expect one so damaged to help you? She's lost to herself now. And it's your fault. You hurt her, and you have made everything worse. Much, much worse!"

I know she is talking about me. The desperation in the bloodless face makes me tremble. I am standing in cold again – wet, dense, bone-cracking cold.

"Nikos," she continues, "why did you go without me? Why didn't you come? How will I ever know what happened?" She begins to cry, terrible choking sobs.

I touch my fingers to my cheeks and feel wetness.

On numb feet I step back, and Thea's short-cropped head appears, bandage and all, behind the potent energy in the mirror. I lift one hand, and Thea's hand rises. Thea. Me? Then who is this other girl? Is she Thea's dream girl come to life somehow? Is it ...

"Susannah?"

Our eyes lock, and I realize that this is the face that floated above me yesterday, the face pressed against the gossamer fabric – the girl in Wilton's study. The same eyes, shadowed and huge, the same full mouth, twisted now in bitterness. But then her shape wavers slightly and the long hair grows dark and limp. To my amazement murky water drips from it and from the now soiled cotton and ribbons of her blouse, yet the floor around her remains perfectly dry.

She speaks in a hollow distant voice. "You see how it was for me? I waited. And this is what happened. I am sorry for your troubles. I don't know if I can change things.

It's surely too late. But I have to try … to stay a bit longer. You must help me. I have to know."

"Have to know what?" I ask, my voice small.

The girl's figure begins to shatter, like still water that's suddenly disturbed. "I think he has come back. I feel him near me. He must be here. Why can't I talk to him? I have to know!"

The figure is dissolving quickly now. Her face hangs in front of me as light and thin as the sheer fabrics above us.

"Know what?" I cry. "Susannah!"

The face evaporates and the whisper is faint, but each word hits me like a slap across the face.

"Why he left me to die."

CHAPTER SIXTEEN

Dazed with misery and shock, I leave the house and wander through the garden and end up in the cemetery standing over the broken headstone. There is something about this grave. I'm sure now it was Susannah I saw standing in this very spot yesterday.

When I grab the top of the headstone, a deep cold sears my hands, making my wrists ache. But I hang on and it slowly turns over with a gentle plop.

The letters are cut deep into the stone:

SUSANNAH BEATRICE LEVER
BELOVED DAUGHTER OF
SAMUEL LEVER
VICAR OF THIS PARISH
BORN JUNE 5, 1911
DIED 1929

The breeze sighs through the leaves. "Yes ... yes ..."

I was right. Susannah was a real person. And the man in the study's picture was her father. Why am I seeing them? How can she be beneath this tombstone *and* in my room?

Does this mean she isn't a figment of my imagination? If not, *what* is she?

There is a full birthdate on the stone, but Susannah's death is marked only by the year – 1929. Nearby gravestones show the day and month for both. Why doesn't hers? I do some quick calculating. She was only eighteen. How did she die? Instinctively I flinch. Maybe she's not dead.

Churches keep records. Would they know about Susannah and her father? Would anyone be there?

I walk quickly to the front of the stone building. A station wagon is parked in the graveled lot. The church door, heavy wood studded with huge nail heads, is not locked. Inside is a small entrance hall. Two french doors stand open showing a carpeted aisle running between rows of polished pews.

Someone is humming – a man's voice – deep and warbly. It echoes in the vast space of the church. A loud thump is followed by "Confound and blast!" and these are followed by low mutterings. Soon the humming begins again. It's coming from a small alcove near the back of the church.

"Hello?" My voice flies up to the rafters.

"Just a minute," a voice calls cheerily from the alcove. "I'll be right there – No, you come here. You sound young and strong, and I could do with a hand."

I peek through heavy curtains covering the arch of the alcove. A very small, very round man dressed all in black is wrestling with an enormous concrete birdbath. There are pieces of wood, cardboard, plastic bubble sheets and heavy flat cord spread around the floor.

The man pushes at the birdbath. It doesn't move. Red-faced, he beams at me over its wide flat top. "Thea, my dear! How are you? My sexton has a cold. I have two christenings tomorrow, and just in case Robert continues to be poorly I must see that everything is prepared."

I'm stunned. "You – you know me?"

He leans his elbows on the edge of the font. "Well, we've only met once officially – when Robert marched you into the church to be chastised for riding your bike through the cemetery. But I knew you were always careful to avoid damaging anything, so we talked of other things. A few days later you had your accident. I had thought to go to the hospital to visit you, but your parents didn't want to confuse you with more strange faces. How are you, my dear?"

"Not bad, I guess."

He looks at me closely. "Really?"

"No, that's not true. It's all a mess. I ... my memory ... it's ..."

"Yes. I know. I did get that much information from your parents. I am sorry, Thea. Can I help you in some way?"

"I – I wanted to ask you about someone whose grave is in this cemetery."

"Oh? Well, when it comes to the history of this place, you've come to the right man. I fancy myself a bit of a local historian. Who is it you're wondering about? No, wait. First I'd like to get this thing set up and then we can sit down and talk properly. How's that?"

"Okay."

"Can you give me a hand shifting it? Are you capable of doing anything physical yet? I wouldn't want –"

"No problem. Just tell me where you want the birdbath put."

He hoots. "Birdbath? It's supposed to be my new 'lightweight marbleized high-tech font' for baptisms. They sent this instead. I'll complain, but no doubt this birdbath will still be here fifty years from now." He wrestles with it again, his round face as red as a pin-cherry.

"It'll scrape the wood floor," I say. "If we tuck a few sheets of cardboard under it maybe it'll slide more easily."

"Of course! You're brilliant, Thea!"

After some fiddling with the cardboard, we manage to move the thing with only a little shoving and yanking. Even so, my head throbs when we're done.

"Oh, my goodness. You're as pale as a ghost! What have I done!" the old man cries. "Isabelle will crown me for putting you to work. I'm Reverend Pikeskill, by the way. Come along, little one. Hot sweet tea for you."

I follow him through a door and up a short flight of stairs into a small office crammed with heavy mahogany furniture. Books cover every inch of the walls, including two shelves over the doorway. In the middle of the desk sits a small blue-and-white cooler and a Thermos.

He guides me to a leather chair, hands me a cup with a saucer and pours tea into it from the Thermos. On a napkin he puts half a chicken sandwich and a jam-filled cookie with bright pink icing. Then he sits down behind the desk, pours tea for himself, beams at me and bites into the other half of the sandwich.

The slightly bulging eyes are a clear intelligent hazel behind wire-rimmed glasses. His hair is a bushy ring of reddish gray with a few thin strands carefully combed over the shiny scalp. I decide his color is a gentle warm brown.

"Eat. Enjoy."

I am suddenly ravenous. I wolf down everything while he tells me that he runs three churches in the district, but this is his favorite.

"Next year they're selling the smallest church, just across the river. They want to sell this one, too. But I'm fighting to keep it going. It was built in 1820, very old indeed for this part of the country. I have the Manitoba Historical Society involved, so I'll no doubt be called devious and subversive by the diocese. Still, I'm determined that if I'm to guide one church into the twenty-first century, it will be this one."

"That's good," I say, not really caring, and brush cookie crumbs off my skirt. Should I talk to him about Susannah? How can I ask him about her and her father without telling him about my hallucinations – or that her thoughts are in my head sometimes, or that I don't remember Thea – but sometimes I think I *am* Susannah. I can't say these things.

He'll think I'm, yeah, nuts.

"About your amnesia, Thea," he says, as if reading my mind. "Are any old memories coming back to you?"

I almost laugh out loud. Just how old does he want? As far back as 1929? "A few seem to be coming back, but in a weird way ..."

"Weird? Like what?"

I can't tell him. "It doesn't matter. What I really want to ask you is whether you know anything about a Susannah Lever. She used to live in the vicarage, I think."

The bright pink cheeks lose their color as if someone has just opened a tap and let his blood drain out.

I lean forward. "You know who I'm talking about?"

"As a matter of fact, Thea, I do, but ..." He rubs short square fingers over his mouth. "Let me think a minute, my dear."

I wait. The silence is broken only by the faint twitter of birds through an open window.

He stares at his hands for what seems like hours. Then abruptly he lets out a deep gusty breath.

"I do know something about a Susannah Lever, but it isn't pleasant. Why do you ask about her in particular?"

"What do you mean, it isn't pleasant?"

"We lived in your house once — my wife, Isabelle, and I. I'm an avid gardener and I thought it would be a great challenge to bring that garden back to its former glory. Someone had clearly laid it out with great care."

What's he going on about? What does this have to do with Susannah. "When did you live there?"

"We moved in during the spring of 1972 and stayed almost two years."

That would make it 1974. Not even close to the year she died. I grit my teeth and listen.

"During that time I managed to clear most of the weeds. Later ... I regretted leaving the garden, but Isabelle was adamant. She wanted to move. Since then the vicarage has been leased a number of times over the years. None of the tenants has ever really looked after the garden, but weeds were pulled now and again, so it didn't go completely wild. Even so, half of me regretted never seeing it the way it must have looked once. And the other half was sorry I'd ever laid eyes on it."

He stares off into the past, his face very sad, and suddenly I know that something dreadful happened in the old vicarage when Susannah was there. I can feel the blood speed up in my veins.

"Why did you move out?" I ask. "Why didn't you stay? *I'm* trying to clear the weeds now. Shouldn't I be? What happened there?"

He smiles. "Oh, it's okay for *you*, my dear. For me it was different. I was the first serious gardener the place had had since 1929 or thereabouts. Or the unluckiest. My predecessor lived there for more than forty years, but he was a terrible gardener. Mowed the lawns, he said, and tidied up as best he could. The church couldn't afford professional gardeners of course. Not like others in the neighborhood."

I want to scream at him to get on with it, but I bite my bottom lip and wait.

He looks into my eyes, assessing. "I'm so sorry, my dear. I've forgotten about your plight in my own selfish meanderings. But maybe I'd better not —"

My hand slams down on the desk. The noise is shattering in the stillness and startles both of us.

"But you must! I have to know!"

"Yes. Yes, of course. Please calm yourself, my dear. It's hard for me to talk about this, you see."

I sit back in my chair and wait.

After a few moments' silence, he says, "It still comes to me as clear as yesterday even though it was more than twenty years ago. So tragic. So young. Poor girl."

Panic flutters in me as if one of the birds outside has begun to beat its wings inside my chest.

"What happened?" I croak.

"I disturbed ... her final rest. You see, one day — in the garden — I found the bones of young Susannah Lever."

CHAPTER SEVENTEEN

"You found her bones? In the garden?" My voice is high and shrill.

"Yes. In the garden."

"But ... how did she get there? And how did you know who she was?"

"Her father, Reverend Lever, was vicar long before my time, but I searched for information about him after the body was found. My immediate predecessor, Reverend Gallagher, moved here permanently right after Reverend Lever left. Gallagher stayed, as I said, for over forty years. He told me there had been a misfortune in the life of Reverend Samuel Lever. His daughter, just a teenager, supposedly ran away with her fiance. Very odd, everyone thought at the time. You see, it was her father who'd arranged her marriage — to a church member who happened to rent the brick house next to the vicarage. The mother had died giving birth, so Susannah was all her father had. He was very protective of her."

"She ran away with the man she was engaged to marry?"

"That's what was believed, yes. Apparently Lever forced

events because he had second thoughts about the engagement and tried to stop the marriage."

"Why?"

"As far as I could tell the young fellow talked of moving out West, and that would mean Lever would lose his only family. This wasn't just a loving parent's concern for his daughter – he had a selfish motive as well. The old man suffered from a mental illness, referred to at that time as "religious mania," and the girl, Susannah, was the only one who could take care of him properly during these dreadful times. But we don't really know if he intended to stop the wedding or not – it's all old gossip."

I remember Papa's wild eyes and my stomach lurches.

"You mean her father was crazy?"

"According to Gallagher, these bouts of mania came and went. He said that Samuel Lever was certain that God was going to test him, and he focused this obsession on his daughter, believing that God was going to test him through her. Perhaps her running away just confirmed this belief – to him, anyway."

"But she didn't run away."

He shakes his head sadly. "No. No, it appears not."

Susannah's words pulse painfully beneath my bandage. *He left me to die.*

"She was murdered," I say.

He sits forward with a jerk. "What gives you that idea, Thea? We don't know how it happened or who buried her or why. True, there were signs of violence on the body, but –"

I swallow hard. "Violence?"

"I called the police of course. Their lab said that her skull was cracked, as if hit from behind. Of course we had no idea who she was for a few days — until I was shown her effects."

In a tiny voice, I say, "Her effects? You mean like clothing? How? It must have been years and years ..."

"About forty-five." Reverend Pikeskill leans back and his voice lowers. "You see, I began on the garden the year I moved in, and it was starting to look better by the time winter came. At least the perennials had room to breathe. The next big job would be the pond. It's surprisingly deep and the stones needed re-laying. My research told me it had once had a splendid fountain, and I found the pipes — fine copper ones — leading underground from the house. I could turn the taps, but nothing happened. I figured after all these years the fountain outlet was simply plugged up."

"Plugged? Was she ... ? Was it her?"

"No, no. I drained it and found it was indeed just stopped up with years of silt and dirt. But when I was dragging the muck out I found a large flat locket. The picture inside was ruined. But —"

"It was Susannah's," I say.

"Yes. Exactly. On the back of it was engraved, 'To Susannah Beatrice Lever from her father on the occasion of her confirmation, 1925.' I assumed she'd lost it while working in the garden. Reverend Gallagher heard she was an avid gardener."

I'm not surprised. Who else could have created the beautiful formal garden I see in my dreams?

"How do you know she died in 1929?" I ask.

"We think it was 1929 because that's when her father left — a shattered man, according to Reverend Gallagher. Gallagher told me the diocese had requested that he take up the post immediately because Susannah's father was struggling with the absence of his daughter, and his work was suffering. Susannah hadn't been gone more than a couple of months when Lever had a complete breakdown and was sent to a church hospital back East. He left a message for her with Gallagher — in case she came back. She never did."

"And when did you find …" I can't say it.

"I found her body not long after I found the locket. You see, I wanted to replace the old garden shed. Behind it was a pile of stones I wanted to add to the rock garden near the house. So I started with the stones first. I had to dig some of them out because many had sunk deep in the soil and … that's when I found it — her. The police said she'd been wrapped in an old rug. There wasn't much left, poor child, just shreds of clothing and bones. The shed is still there, I believe."

The room is receding. I am sinking, sinking. A glass is pressed to my lips, liquid fire in my mouth. I come to the surface with a jolt.

"Scotch. Medicinal," Reverend Pikeskill says, patting my icy fingers, as I cough and cough.

I wave the glass away.

He crouches beside me and I hear his knees pop. "I keep making things worse, don't I? And you've been ill. I shouldn't have told you. Isabelle will skin me alive."

I shake my head and find my voice. "No, no. I'm glad you did. But you still haven't told me what made you, uh, identify the body as my – Susannah's."

"There was a bracelet in the grave. The same filigreed silver as the locket. Her initials were on it. There was no one else it could have been. The police coroner determined that the body was that of a young woman."

"Did he ever figure out exactly what happened to her?"

"Well, he pretty well confirmed that the injury to the skull caused her death."

A cold hand squeezes my heart. So she *is* dead. Her bones lie buried in the graveyard. Then why do I still see her?

"They didn't have much luck talking to people after all those years," Reverend Pikeskill continues. "Many of the congregation were either dead or had moved away or were too young to remember the Levers. I did talk to one very old woman, a former organist and choir leader, Miss Pym, who remembered when Susannah disappeared. Apparently, Susannah didn't take much part in the social events of the community – only church events. Typical of a minister's family at the time. Besides, she had a house to run. You can imagine how her so-called running away caused quite a scandal."

"A scandal?"

"Yes, of course – a furtive fleeing in the night. No white

wedding in the church. Miss Pym remembered the last sermon Lever gave. She said he was crazy as a coot, screaming from the pulpit about vipers in the garden and about how people had to protect their daughters. He was led from the church still raving. Miss Pym knew him quite well, and became terribly upset retelling the story even after all these years."

"And was it because of that last sermon that everyone found out about Susannah running away?"

"Yes, and there's the point, you see. People wanted to know *why* Susannah felt she had to leave. Miss Pym verified my guess that there was a man involved. She thought it *may* have been Susannah's fiance. He definitely left town around that time, according to her, taking all his belongings with him – papers, clothing, everything. The parish was all a-twitter, she said – buzzing with a different rumor – that the girl had actually run away with the gardener who *worked* for her fiance. And that the fiance had left town because he was so embarrassed at being jilted."

My scalp tightens. The name I heard in the cottage. "The gardener ... was his name Nikos?"

The vicar looks at me intently. "Miss Pym didn't know. He was a bit of a mystery – quiet, hardworking. She knew a bit more about the fiance. He apparently came from an upper-class family in England and had a private income. No one knew for sure what he did with his time. In any case, he showed up in the community one day, joined the church and seemed quite popular, even though he, too, was a bit of a loner. Miss Pym said it was just *assumed* that he and Susannah left to get away from her father's demands on her."

"But she didn't go anywhere," I remind him.

"Yes. You know, at the time I remember thinking, what if her fiance found out about the gardener and her? Would he be jealous? Could he be the one – ?"

"Who killed her?" The pulsing in my head grows stronger, thump, thump, thump, like the anger of the thin-faced man in the garden. Was *he* the fiance? He talked about a wedding date between himself and Susannah. It must be him. "*Is* he the one who killed her?" I repeat.

Reverend Pikeskill stammers, "Well – I, er, it seemed more than a coincidence that they, uh, disappeared on the same day. But perhaps he ran away after she was ... well, you know."

I rub damp hands down my shorts. "What was his name?"

He frowns. I can't wait. I jump in. "Was it Fitzgerald? Jeremy Fitzgerald?"

"I don't think I ever found out. But, Thea, how would *you* know?"

I stare at him. How *would* I know? I'm certain that the name Fitzgerald is important. But the boy next door is also named Fitzgerald, and he couldn't possibly have had anything to do with Susannah's death. Why did hearing the name make me faint last night? I grit my teeth. I'll find out – everything. About this Nikos person. About the man called Jeremy. About the name Fitzgerald.

And especially about Susannah Beatrice Lever.

CHAPTER EIGHTEEN

Reverend Pikeskill breaks into my thoughts. "Thea. Something more than simple curiosity brought you here. I will keep it strictly confidential. I don't wish to pry, so if you want to keep it to yourself ..."

I come to a decision. "Do you believe in dead people coming back to life?"

"Do you mean as ghosts? Are you telling me you're seeing spirits?"

"I don't know. I'm not sure. Sometimes I see and hear things, and I'm sure it's my imagination. Other times I'm sure these things are real. I don't *know* what's real and what isn't. I think, before the accident, Thea – that is, *I* – made things up and probably got carried away. Maybe I just *heard* about Susannah and her father and made up a little world around them and that's what I'm remembering ... seeing – *imaginary* people. I don't know!" I touch my bandage with shaky fingertips.

"When was the last time you had that looked at?" he asks. "The bandage is grubby, if you don't mind my saying."

I'm so surprised I laugh.

His eyes twinkle. "The living must be looked after first."

I'm sure he doesn't believe me, but at least he hasn't said so or acted strange about it.

"Wait here." He's gone only a minute, returning with a first-aid kit. "We usually have one or two skinned knees a week with all that gravel out there." He gently lifts the bandage off my skin.

"Mmm. Clean as a whistle. And healing nicely. I think an even smaller bandage will do the trick."

I nod. "I have to get home. The girls will be back soon, and I'm responsible —"

"Your parents said they missed your help."

My stomach tightens. "Yeah. I'll bet."

"Thea, about your ... problem. I haven't ignored you. I've been giving it some serious thought. It's possible — just possible, mind — that you're registering something paranormal. Something that has to do with Susannah Lever."

"Paranormal?"

"There are a few of us in the church who have seen some very strange things and heard strange tales from parishioners. A number of our members also belong to the British Society of Psychical Research, a venerable organization that believes there is something happening between the world of the living and those who have passed on, and that sometimes the dead do communicate with the living. Especially when something violent has happened."

"Like Susannah being murdered?"

"Well, if she met a violent death the negative energy

might still be there and somehow you're ... bumping into it — and it envelops you, pulls you in. As you get better it should eventually stop. Until then you have to, well, carry on with your own life as best you can."

If I wasn't so scared I'd laugh out loud. Carry on with *what* life?

"It — it's only happened a few times," I tell him, "and I'm not sure anything really ... *happened*."

He taps my hand with one finger. "If you need help — when you feel you *must* have help — I'll be here. You may have to put up with these strange occurrences for a while before you know what's actually happening. But I won't abandon you." He digs around in his pocket and hands me a card. "My home number. Call any time. I'll fill Isabelle in. I'm here in the church from ten till two every day — except for events like birdbath arranging in the other churches." He smiles.

"Thanks."

"Did the doctors talk to you about your amnesia and its possible side-effects?" he asks.

"Not much. I had to have an operation to drain off fluid, but Dr. Browning said my memory will come back in time."

"The mind is an amazing thing, Thea. They put a bandage on to protect the incision on the outside of your head, but sometimes people need a bandage over a deeper wound. Perhaps that's partly what all this is about. Your amnesia could be a bandage you've put on until you're ready to look at what hurt you — deep down. These other things — these spirits — could be part of it, too."

"But how will I know what it is?"

"You'll know — in time. It might be a whole series of things that were building up inside before the accident."

I smile sadly. "Or it might just be from a bonk on the head."

He smiles back. "Or maybe just a bonk."

"I have to go."

"Trust your instincts in regards to things that seem to be happening, my dear. I don't think you have anything to fear from these events. The air has a thousand voices. You'll have to learn to listen to the right one."

I look at him blankly.

He smiles. "Try not to worry, eh? Call me. Even if all you want to do is gripe about the family."

He's not fobbing me off — I know he means it. "Okay, thanks."

But how can he really *understand?*

We walk through the chapel together and he opens the big door for me.

"I hope you get to keep your church," I say.

There is a hint of steel in the gentle eyes. "I'm a fighter. Remember that, Thea. I'll fight for you if you need me, too. You're not alone."

"I'll try to remember."

I walk through the graveyard feeling stronger than I have since the accident. As I draw near Susannah's final grave, I keep my eyes on the path, but as the flickering shadows close in, dark and brooding, fears grow and twist inside me and I know that I *am* alone — completely and utterly alone.

CHAPTER NINETEEN

It's past seven o'clock and The Parents aren't home yet. The girls and I are at the kitchen table. I've hardly listened to their arguing, the core of my mind is so preoccupied by my talk with Reverend Pikeskill.

Is the house haunted? The garden too? He called it "negative energy" and said it should eventually stop. Could he be wrong? Could this place *stay* haunted unless I do something about it? But what?

Things in this world seem diluted and growing thinner, as if an oily darkness is sliding just below the surface, threatening to seep through and engulf everything, including me.

My escape from the gloom of the graveyard and the race across the darkening garden has left me with the taste of fear. And yet there's still that part of me that sees everything as an observer. No emotional response. Assessing. Watching. Sorting. I find a curious comfort in this passionless Thea.

"Big fire. Black pot. Big noisy fire engines," I hear Wee say.

Her words catch my attention. "You had a fire? Here? When?"

Ellie cries, "See? I told you she wasn't listening. It wasn't a real fire. Jeez, I told Mama and Daddy and the police and the firemen and everyone. I was making popcorn and forgot the oil for a second or two and it caught fire. I put it out with salt, just like the fireman said who came to our school. I have a very retentive memory." She jabs her temple with a finger. "There was only a bit of smoke damage. And for that I can't use the stove anymore. Pul-lease!"

"Ellie not allowed." Wee's enjoying the power. "So no dinner."

"Well, we have to eat. There's no Kraft Dinner," Ellie says, "but I could make sloppy macaroni. Thea won't remember how."

"No stove!" Wee says firmly.

"Oh, shut up."

"Never mind, Wee," I say. "We're all starving. What's this sloppy-macaroni stuff?"

"It's *your* invention," Ellie says.

"Well, I don't remember. *Remember?*"

"I can't use the stupid stove, so what's the difference?"

"Tell me what to do and I can try it," I say. "Or maybe there's something in one of those cookbooks. Or maybe, I could allow you to use the stove."

Her eyes narrow. "So you can squeal on me later?"

"Squeal? To The Parents? You've got to be joking. Now, how do you make this stuff?"

Ellie purses her upper lip into a little point and says, "Okay. To make this particular dish, you boil water madly and then throw in two teacups of dried macaroni and you boil it and boil it until it gets soft. Then you drain it and leave a bit of water at the bottom and then you throw in one teacup of that dry cheese in the green carton and then you serve it up." She blinks around smugly.

"Sounds okay," I say. "But shouldn't you have vegetables or something with it? The only decent meal the hospital kitchen made was macaroni and cheese with veggies."

Wee opens the fridge door and peers in. "Green trees. Yuck."

"She means broccoli," Ellie explains, taking a look. "And there's some of that tofu stuff."

"Tofu?" I ask.

"It's made out of soybeans. Kinda like soft plastic cheese with no flavor," Ellie says. "You cut it into little blocks and put it in tomato sauce and stuff."

"Yuck! Yuck! Yuck!" Wee cries.

"And there're two wieners in the freezer."

"Okay. Take them out. Any regular cheese?" I ask, pushing the girls aside. "Look. Here's a little chunk of cheddar. Let's get to work."

Wee pulls apart the green trees, Ellie cuts up the wieners, and I set to work boiling water and grating cheese.

When the macaroni is ready, I drain it, throw in everything else and stir it around. The cheese and noodles form a big lump on the bottom.

We stare down into the pot.

"Water," says Wee.

"No," Ellie butts in. "Add some milk and then put it on the stove again and it'll all melt in."

"Good idea. I think the wieners are still a bit frozen," I say.

I add half a carton of milk and eventually everything melts down. Most of the macaroni has shredded into little bits, and the bottom of the pot is dark and crusty brown. Very gourmet.

We cut bread, pour apple juice and sit down to platefuls of steaming goo.

"I think we should call this something," I say, poking my pile with a fork.

"How about too-hungry-to-care stew?" suggests Ellie.

"Mmm, good," says Wee, her mouth full.

I try it. "The trees taste better than I thought they would."

"And the tree stumps aren't bad either," says Ellie, holding up a broccoli stem. "I think that I will never see a stew as lovely as this tree! We had a poem like that in school."

We laugh and spray cheese and bits of macaroni onto the plastic tablecloth, which makes us laugh even harder. But then the kitchen door slams open, and Agatha struggles through carrying a large flat box.

"You're eating?" she says. "For heaven's sake! I told Germaine to tell you it was my night to do dinner. I bought a pizza. Well! That was a waste of twenty-some dollars." She drops the box in the middle of the table with a loud slap.

The door swings open behind her. Wilton stares around with a bemused smile. "Good. You're eating dinner. I'm famished. Good grief! What is it?"

"We make it!" Wee crows. "I do little trees. Good!"

"You let her use a sharp knife?" Agatha says to me accusingly.

"Agatha. Why is there a pizza box on the table?" Wilton asks.

"I couldn't get away —"

"You mean *you're* just getting home, too? I thought we agreed —"

"Well, *you* didn't make it home on time *once* when Thea was in the hospital," Agatha snarls, "so don't start —"

"I beg your pardon, but I went to see our daughter almost every afternoon between classes," Wilton says. "And, uh, what does that have to do with your not preparing dinner tonight?"

"Well, I had to sit in on that conference this afternoon about the Samaritans. And I have to get right back for the final session. I came home just to get these kids a meal, so don't tell me —"

"It *was* your turn, Aggie, and as I said, we agreed —"

"So that gives *you* the right not to come home until now, I suppose," she says, glaring at him. "I tried to call you at work, but you weren't there. Probably at the pub with —"

"That's totally untrue, Aggie! I was —"

"Shut up!" I shout.

There is a stunned silence. Wee hides her face in her arms and begins to whimper.

"Look at what you've done, Thea!" Agatha pats Wee's shoulder.

"Oh, the concerned mother!"

"Now hold on, hold on," says Wilton. "That's hardly fair. Why, your mother —"

"My mother? I can't believe she's *anyone's* mother. It's just as well I *don't* remember her. Or you. Why —"

Agatha interrupts. "What is *that* supposed to mean?"

"Exactly what I said. I'm glad I don't remember either of you. The way you treat these kids is … is *disgusting*."

"How dare you!" Agatha cries.

"I had to shampoo Wee's hair yesterday because it stunk. *She* stunk. Ellie takes pretty good care of herself, because she's older, but I've seen holes in her socks so big both heels stick out!"

"Thea, I'm warning you …"

"Do they ever get a decent meal? Do you ever read them a bedtime story? What kind of life will this new baby have? Or will I be expected to bring it up while you're rushing around helping everyone except your own family?"

"You see?" Agatha says almost triumphantly, turning to Wilton. "She hasn't changed at all. Still as mouthy and opinionated as ever."

"What do you mean?" I demand.

"Deadly silence and sulks or telling us dire things would happen if we didn't do this or that for you and the girls. And all done with one limp hand dramatically over your brow. You haven't changed a bit."

Blood rushes into my cheeks. I speak slowly and loudly. "I feel sorry for the Thea I'm *supposed* to have been. You say she ... I haven't changed. Then you whisper about my *mental* state, how unstable I am, but you wouldn't come to the doctor's with me! And you haven't even bothered to ask what happened at the appointment today. You don't know, but –"

Agatha sucks in a weary breath. "You didn't give us a chance!"

"Face it, you're just worried about how long it's going to take before I can get back to doing all your work for you!"

"Now, Thea, let's be reasonable," Wilton says, his eyes huge behind the thick glasses. "We don't believe you're, uh, unstable, as you put it. And we don't expect you to do –"

"I heard you. Whining about how you couldn't miss any more work and how it was going to take forever for me to get better!"

Agatha's swollen face is pasty white. "You were eavesdropping on Wilton and me."

"Yeah, I was. So what?"

"Well, you obviously missed the part where we talked about the fear you must be going through. The sense of loss. I've spent hours searching medical journals – to try and help you. There's almost nothing out there about traumatic amnesia."

I stare at her, thinking hard. Is she telling the truth?

"Certainly it's hard on all of us," she continues. "I would be lying if I denied that, but you must understand –"

I smile bitterly. "Oh, I understand. I definitely understand."

She rubs her temples with her fingertips. "Look, I'm sorry. Thea. I have so *much* to think about. All I ask is for some help around here. I can't do it on my own! I can't do it without you. Of course I wish you'd never had that bloody accident. Yes. I wish, wish, *wish* you were Thea again —"

"Aggie!" Wilton says, aghast.

She turns on him. "Don't you Aggie me! How can I get through this? I have so much work to do. And you, you're always at school or locked in your study —"

"Aggie, come on, now." Wilton's arms hang at his sides. "I know how important your work is, but we made a decision about the baby — together. Maybe you should —"

"I should what? Think about quitting work? I don't imagine *you'd* think about cutting down on your night classes."

Wilton tries to catch a look at his watch.

"See? You've got extra classes tonight. But I'm supposed to let *my* work go. My group was just getting to a critical point tonight and —"

I lift the pizza box off the table. "Wee. Ellie. We'll eat this in my room."

I swallow hard, fighting the tears that grab at my throat. The girls troop out in front of me. At the door I stare back at The Parents. They really are pathetic.

"You'd better get this sorted out," I say. "Thea's not your servant anymore."

CHAPTER TWENTY

In the darkening light in my room, the girls and I chew at the edges of the pizza. The house is quiet after all the slamming of car doors and roaring of engines as The Parents left. Very mature of them.

"You sure got mad," Ellie says. "Does this mean you're going away soon?"

"Why? Is that what you want?"

She drops her half-eaten slice of pizza back into the carton. "I just want to know when you're going, that's all."

"Who said I'm going anywhere?"

Wee throws herself on me and squashes tomato sauce on my shorts.

"Thea no go!"

I glare at Ellie over the kid's head. "Why are you doing this? You know it gets Wee all riled up."

She shrugs. "I'm going to bed. I've got a stomach ache."

"Take Wee with you."

"Take her yourself. When you go, I'll probably get stuck with her all the time."

Wee squeals and whines, "No, no! Thea no —"

"Okay, okay, take it easy. Thanks a lot, Ellie," I call to the skinny back as it disappears down the hall.

I take Wee to her bedroom and help her into a pair of pajamas. I try to convince her I need a night to myself and promise I won't sneak away while she's sleeping. I finally wear the kid down and she sags onto her pillow, her thumb tucked in her mouth.

As I approach Ellie's room I hesitate. Should I talk to her about scaring Wee? When I open her door a crack I hear a snuffling sound and a low moan.

The room is dim, except for a small bedside lamp. Sitting cross-legged in the middle of a narrow bed is Ellie, her hands pressed to her face. She's making terrible gulping sounds.

Should I sneak back out? The door creaks and I'm caught. Quickly wiping her eyes with her pajama sleeve, she mutters, "What do you want? My room is off limits."

"What's up? Why are you crying?"

"I'm not crying."

"Looks and sounds like crying to me."

"What do you know? You don't have a mind."

"Thanks very much. You and your parents agree on that."

"I'm not like them! Go away."

I sit on the end of her bed. "Did you and I hate each other this much before?"

She blinks at me through red-rimmed eyes. "I never hated you. And you only started acting weird a few weeks before the accident."

"Weird?"

"Yeah. Talking about running away, so Mama and Daddy would have to act like real parents. You really meant to do it. And then when you had your accident I thought maybe you'd be glad to be home. But now you hate it here even worse than before. I bet you'll go and maybe even take Wee with you." Her voice starts to shake. "And I'll be all alone. You always leave me out of things."

"I thought you wanted me to go, with or without Wee."

"I ... I didn't ever want you to go. You ... you're the only one who ever helps me with things."

"Things?"

"When you weren't being mad at everyone you helped me with my homework, and with ... you know, boys and stuff. And you'd let me come shopping with you. And we were even starting to go to movies together. I don't have a really good friend at school. I'm too –" she searches for the word "– caustic. That's what you called me. You were going to help me make friends and ... stuff."

"And if I go?"

"If you go, I'll have to do everything alone. I won't have anyone to talk to. I thought when your memory came back we'd be kind of like ... friends again."

"Kind of?"

She smiles a watery smile. "We had lots of fights, but ... well, it didn't mean we didn't ... you know ..."

"Yeah, I know. Listen, Ellie. I couldn't leave now even if I wanted to. I have nowhere to go. No money. And like you said – no brain, either."

She dashes the tears away with the flat of her hands. "You won't? Really?"

"Really. Besides, we've got to sort out The Parents, don't we?"

"I don't think they'll ever change."

I sigh. "Maybe not. But I'll stick around for a while yet."

A worried frown creases her forehead below the tangle of black hair. "But maybe, one day, you'll go?"

"We'll both be going one day, won't we? In a few years we'll be grown up and we'll leave. Right?"

Her face clears. "Yeah ... that's right!"

"You better get to sleep."

She rummages around in the mess of covers and pulls them over her. "Okay. Are you going to be awake for a while? Maybe reading or something?"

"You want me to stay until you get to sleep?"

"You don't have to stay here." Her voice has that sharp edge again. "I'm not a baby."

"Right. Well, I'd planned to read for a bit, anyway. See you tomorrow."

For the first time she smiles at me as if she means it.

My bedroom is hot. I push the window open wider, change into a T-shirt nightie and lie on top of the covers. Funny, my relationship with Ellie has changed in less than an hour. I feel guilty for not picking up on the reasons for her hurt feelings sooner. And what about my feelings? Is Wee the only one who cares about mine? I don't know if The Parents care about me or not. Oh, maybe Wilton feels guilty, but Agatha? Who knows? What with her pregnancy and my accident and her work, maybe she doesn't have time to feel anything.

It slowly dawns on me – I have real memories now. Even if it is only one month's worth. Even if a lot of them aren't happy ones. Will the times before the accident ever return? Will they be as painful as tonight's? Will they come back one by one? Or will they crash in all at once?

While I'm collecting new memories every day connected to Thea's family, there are those other memories that frighten me: Susannah's image in the mirror and her whispered words; the vision of black earth being turned over to expose sharp white bones and shreds of clothing; Jeremy's dark angry eyes and sneering mouth; the gentle eyes of the curly-haired man; and the living photograph of Susannah's papa – the obsessed ranting old man Reverend Pikeskill described.

"Go away!" I mutter furiously, swinging my legs over the edge of the bed. I look out the window. The garden is washed in navy blue, the hedges and trees outlined in the moon's faint light.

Like that pallid, translucent circle, I feel as if I'm floating in my own dark lonely world. There's something achingly familiar about this feeling. Does it come from Thea? Or from Susannah?

Purr leaps from the bed onto the windowsill and leans against the screen, staring down at something outside. What if he pushes too hard and falls out the window?

That's all I need, a squashed cat. I am about to order him to get down, when suddenly, lightning threads through the sky like the spectacular roots of a huge tree. In that single flash the garden is clearly visible.

Someone is standing by the pond.

With a high-pitched yowl Purr hurls himself into his hiding place in my wardrobe.

A voice rushes up from below and whirls around my head.

"I'm here!" it calls. "I'm here!"

I lean close to the screen, my eyes searching the darkness. Is it the boy, Lucas Fitzgerald? The moon rides out from behind a cloud, washing everything in indigo and tracing the figure of a short stocky man.

He raises his hands to his mouth and calls again.

Something deep inside me knows that voice. The glow surrounding the figure illuminates the pond and the shimmering tumble of water that floats high in the air behind him. Joy surges through me. I must go to him.

By the time I've reached the kitchen I've changed my mind. Shivering in my nightie, I stand behind the screen door in the unlit kitchen. He's still there, but closer to the house. My scalp prickles. What now? What exactly did I intend to do once I was out there? I can see the breadth of his shoulders and the solid strength of his legs in dark-colored trousers. It's the gentle man with the black curly hair. He beckons to me, then slowly turns and walks past the fountain toward the hedge that separates the two yards. When he disappears into the inky shadows I push the door open with a creak and slip silently out onto the back stoop.

As I debate whether to follow him something moves behind me. I glance back through the screen door, and my insides turn in on themselves. Coming toward me across the kitchen is a tall heavy man with dishevelled silver hair and a face that sags like warm ivory wax. He's dressed all in black except for a white scarf wrapped like a collar that almost touches his ears. I can see the wild mad look in his eyes.

Papa.

I press against cold stone wall, not breathing. He walks right through the screen door as if it doesn't exist, first a leg and then a shimmering hand and then his whole body — straight down the steps and into the garden.

Lightning flashes again, and across the river thunder mutters. Papa stands very still as if listening, then glides across the lawn toward the neighbor's hedge. I creep along behind him, keeping my distance, the grass icy under my bare feet.

When he reaches the opening in the hedge he slides straight through it. I hesitate. What if he's waiting for me on the other side?

I inch my way through the gap and can see the old man's silvery head moving through the moonlight. Holding my breath, I step through to the other side just as someone slips out from behind a tree. It's the one called Jeremy —

the man from the garden seat who yelled at Susannah and me. He smiles a sly satisfied smile, then sinks back into the shadows.

"Hey, you!" I shout. "Wait! What —"

Fingers, hard and cold, clamp over my mouth.

"Don't move," a voice hisses in my ear. "Do you hear me? Don't move."

I nod frantically.

"You've ruined everything," the voice continues. "They've gone!"

Chapter Twenty-one

Three small lights flutter in jam jars on the mantelpiece, and a low fire scatters shadows around the room.

"What's that weird smell?" I ask. "You using drugs?"

Lucas Fitzgerald throws a few more pieces of wood on the fire. Over his shoulder he says, "Essential oils from different flowers. You put them in little rings that float on oil with a candle wick. I keep seeing a garden – flower images, you know? I thought the oils might work. I was right. I don't need drugs – I feel too much and see too much as it is." He stares into the flames.

I kneel beside him, the fire hot on my cold arms. "Who's they? Who were you talking about out there?"

"You know." Flames flicker across his face, casting shadow and light over the narrow planes. "The girl – did you see her?"

"Who do you mean?"

"The girl. Susannah."

"Do *you* see her?" I ask breathlessly.

"Yes. But not tonight. And she can't see *them,* except in her memory. There's one she needs to talk to."

"She does?" I whisper.

He stares into the flames and in a soft voice says, "'And moving thro' a mirror clear that hangs before her all the year, shadows of the world appear. There she sees the highway near, winding down to Camelot ... And sometimes thro' the mirror blue, the knights come riding two and two: She hath no loyal knight and true, the Lady of Shalott.'" He looks at me. "She had no loyal knight. Just an ordinary guy."

"What are you talking about? Do you write poetry?"

"It's part of a poem, but I didn't write it. It comes to me again and again in my head. It was written by someone a long time ago."

"What does it mean?" I ask, hands clenched.

"Well, the Lady of Shalott has been shut away for a very long time, and as the poem goes on, the new love she feels for someone takes her out of her secluded shadows into the real world." He opens his eyes and looks at me again.

"She's secluded in shadows?"

"Yeah. Like you. Like Susannah. Her father was her shadow. Watched her like a hawk, afraid he'd lose her. Of course, that only drove her away. He was sick in his mind and in his heart."

"Wait a minute! How do you know all this? How do you know any of it? About Susannah? Or her father?"

"You wouldn't understand," he says, and looks into the flames.

I can't help myself. I blurt out, "I see her *everywhere*. And now I'm seeing her father, and this other man with a mustache, and still another one – outside the house tonight."

He grabs my wrist. "You've seen her? I wasn't sure you had. And the father and the other one tonight – you saw them?"

"Yes. Are they –"

"Did you see the one with the mustache hiding in the shadows?"

"Y-yes."

Lucas's face is very close to mine, and I see a mixture of relief and dread in the green eyes. His grip tightens. "I don't know who he is. I can't seem to make him fit. But you see him, too?"

I pull my arm away. "Yes. And her. And her father. And tonight I saw –"

"When did you first see her?"

"When I was lying on my bed yesterday. She just appeared, floating above me. And this morning she was in my room staring at herself in the mirror. And she saw me, too, or I thought she did. Then I decided I was completely out of my mind – what there is of it!" I smother a hysterical giggle. "She talks to me, whispers in my ear. I don't always see her, but I can hear her – like she's inside my head. Crazy, huh?"

"You're not crazy. Listen, you're sure she's speaking to *you?*"

"Not all the time. Sometimes she's talking to the others – arguing mostly."

"So that's why I can't hear her very well," he mutters. "She's using you. Before your accident I saw her more often. In the garden. In the cemetery. But never clearly. Then I started seeing her when you were around, but even then she wasn't very distinct."

"With me? You mean following me around?"

"Like your shadow."

I shiver and rub my arms. "How do I make her go away — make *them* go away?"

"You can't. It's my job to figure this all out. Doc told me that I would have to try to keep others safe if something like this happened. I only hope I know how."

"And what does *that* mean? Who's Doc? You're not making sense."

He smiles ruefully. "I've heard that before."

"Is that why you hang around? To keep me safe? From Susannah? From her father? From the man in the garden? Who are they? Are they real?"

The slanted eyes come close. "You have to resist her until I know what she wants."

"But I know what she wants."

"You what?" The whites widen around the green irises.

"I said, I know what she wants. Someone murdered her and she wants to know why he left her there. 'I have to know why he left me to die.' That's what she said."

His face tightens, closing off from me. Then, slowly, it changes. The sharp planes dissolve and mould themselves into rounder fuller features. The straight brown hair grows black and glistening with curls. When the thick lashes open he looks at me with different eyes — large and deep-set.

I know these eyes. I know this face.

My skin flushes hot and the blood pounds thick and slow through my body. Something dreadful — no, something amazing — has happened. The flames zigzag across the broad features. I know him ... I know him.

He moves closer and his lips are cold against my cheek. My eyelids grow heavy. Something inside me drops softly, and when his mouth touches mine my bones dissolve under my skin.

With a crash the door flings open behind us. Wind, leaves, stones and dust burst in on a roaring wind. The shock sucks my breath away, for standing in the door is Papa, his face contorted with fury. He is shouting something, but I can't hear what it is, only loud blasts of rage carried on the wind.

"Papa! No!"

Someone pulls me up by the shoulders and shouts in my face, "Run! Run!" but I can't move. My eyes are riveted on the madman at the door.

The boy, the curly-haired man — together as one person — drag me through the back door, shouting, "Run! Run!"

My muscles are rigid. I can't move. The little house vibrates with the sounds of things smashing all around us.

"Hurry!"

Someone grabs my hand and pulls me into the pitch-blackness of the woods. I stumble over roots and twigs on legs that belong to someone else — sluggish and heavy. Footsteps thud on the wet earth behind us. I see the river shining ahead and suddenly a sizzle of energy sweeps through me and I am running on my own, keeping pace with the boy. Behind me, I hear the slap of feet, nearer and nearer.

When I look back over my shoulder it is the curly-haired man, almost upon us. Beside him, her eyes wide with terror, is Susannah; and just behind them, the glow of her father's white scarf and hair. Someone grabs my shoulder. I scream and fall to my knees.

"Don't stop. Keep going!" Lucas gasps.

On hands and knees we scramble under the bushes, through thick muck and sharp twigs and slimy leaves. There's a clearing a few feet away. I grab Lucas's shirtsleeve and lurch forward, still crouched. With a gasp of horror I drop into thin air, landing on soft wet soil with a *whumph*. Lucas lands right beside me.

"This way," he urges. "I know where we are."

Like a wind-up toy, I crawl behind him. We huddle under an umbrella of roots attached to an enormous tree that leans out over the water. There is silence now, except for our breathing and the slurp of water against the muddy riverbank.

Slowly, over the next few hours, the streetlights across the river grow dim under the spreading light. Morning arrives. And we are alone.

CHAPTER TWENTY-TWO

"I'm afraid," I whisper, staring at the little cottage.

"They've gone — I don't hear them anymore," he says. "It's okay."

Nothing inside has been touched. Ashes lie cold and still in the grate. No broken dishes. No smashed glass.

I gawk around in amazement. "But I thought everything was —"

"This is pretty standard," he says. "All of it happened a long time ago. This was just a kind of replay we got caught up in."

I fight tears of exhaustion. "Were those people real? Are you real? I don't even know for sure if *I'm* real. I don't remember anything before a few weeks ago."

"You will someday."

"How do you know?"

"I just do."

"But I have no memories."

"Yes, you do. You've just locked them away for a while."

"But *why* is all this happening? What does it have to do with me?"

"It's my fault. It started when I came to live here about two weeks before you fell off your bike," he says. "I was there when it happened. She stood up right in front of you that day in the cemetery. I knew you'd hurt yourself bad. I called the ambulance."

"You saw me? Did I know you?"

"I was around, but we hadn't met." His smile is shy. "I wish I'd talked to you. But, well, I haven't talked to many regular people – not for a long time. Anyway, like I said, it's all my fault."

"Will you quit saying that? Maybe my accident triggered all this stuff. Why would anything be your fault?" I demand. "You just work here."

"I was sent here."

"*Sent?* By who?"

"My grandfather. He rented the big house a long time ago."

My scalp tightens like a vice. "Are you going to tell me that your grandfather knew Susannah?"

"That's exactly what I'm telling you. They were engaged for a while."

This is getting crazier and crazier. "And his name's Fitzgerald? Like yours?

"Yes. Jeremy Fitzgerald."

"Jeremy? It can't be, because if it is, then how … Are you saying your grandfather's still alive?"

"Barely. But before he got sick, he told me to look for Susannah."

I stare at him. "He's *alive?* But he'd be ..."

"He's almost ninety."

"And he wants you to find a dead girl he knew all those years ago? This *is* nuts. Besides, how could he be alive and —"

"Look, all Grandpa told me was that Susannah Lever was his fiancee. She was reclusive, shy. He said her whole life was tending her garden, painting and running the house for her father. He was in love with her — I could tell by the way he talked about her."

"She painted?" My voice is high and tight. "Are you sure?"

"That's what he said."

Thea's garden paintings march across my inner vision — the garden planted by Susannah Lever. Did Thea meet Susannah before she had her accident?

"But something happened to Susannah shortly after the engagement," Lucas says.

Is he going to tell me she was murdered? "What?" I ask.

"Grandpa told me that when he and Susannah got to know each other a little, the vicar encouraged them to get married, but only provided she stay nearby to help him out. Susannah told Grandpa she didn't love him, but he hoped she would learn to. And so they got engaged. A gardener-handyman came with the house he rented. I think that's the man we saw last night — the stocky guy with the curly hair."

"Nikos?" I ask eagerly, saying the name I heard from

Susannah's lips.

He looks stunned. "Grandpa said he couldn't remember. But I've heard the name Nikos whispered throughout this cottage. How did you know?"

"I heard it somewhere. Go on."

"Anyway, the gardener and Susannah became friends. I guess Grandpa and the vicar didn't think much about it – two avid gardeners and everything – but it looks like this guy got pretty intense about Susannah."

"And she about him?"

"Not according to my grandfather. He warned Susannah about this man and about keeping her distance, but she just laughed it off. And then one night the guy attacked her."

"Nikos *attacked* her? How?"

"Grandpa wouldn't say. But I've felt the gardener's intense feelings all around me since I got here. This spirit's pain is immense – or maybe it's guilt, I can't always tell. Anyway, after this ... attack or whatever it was, the gardener was fired."

Is Lucas making all this up?

"What happened after she was attacked?"

"Grandpa said she withdrew from everything, including him. So he finally gave up and left after she made it clear she wouldn't marry him. I know she died young – I mean, she ended up in this cemetery, right? And now you say she's looking for whoever killed her. I've sensed violence all around, but nothing clear ever came through. I know something is wrong with Grandpa's story, but I haven't worked out what it is. I wish Doc was here. He'd know. He'd help me channel it better."

"I don't know who this Doc person is or how you can *sense* violence, but one part of your grandfather's story is definitely wrong. The gardener loved Susannah. And I don't believe he would've hurt her. But one person who *could* have hurt her – killed her – was your grandfather."

The silence beats in the room like a third heart.

CHAPTER TWENTY-THREE

"How can you say that? You don't know my grandfather!" Lucas's voice is low and harsh.

"Maybe I do," I mutter.

"What?"

"You say he's not dead. That he's sick. Are you sure he's still alive?"

"I'm sure. A few weeks after I got here he went into a coma. I talked to the nurses yesterday. He's barely holding his own, but he's alive."

My chest tightens. Maybe I've got it all wrong. How could he be an old man, still alive, and a young man in the garden at the same time? It's impossible. There has to be another explanation.

"The man with the mustache was hanging around out here last night, watching Susannah's papa when he stormed toward the cottage ..." I search for the best way to tell him.

"What *about* him? I've seen him a couple of times, but like I said before I can't fit him in with the others. It's as if he's an observer."

"You don't recognize him?"

"Should I?"

"I thought ..." I chew my lip, then decide. "Yes, I'm sure it's him. Susannah said his name when he was yelling at her."

"Who?" His eyes widen.

"Your grandfather. Jeremy."

"What? But how ..."

I tell him about my encounter with the young man in the garden. "He said something like, 'You are to be my wife. You can't live in some fantasy world with that foreign creature.' And then he said he'd fired him."

"I don't understand. How could he –"

"It was him! The guy with the mustache and smooth black hair. He was furious, shouting at Susannah, barely keeping in control. I thought he was a real live person at first, but then he vanished right in front of me. I convinced myself I'd imagined him. But I'm certain he was the same man we saw in the shadows of the trees last night."

"He can't be my grandfather."

"Who else could it be? She called him by name – Jeremy."

Lucas looks as if he's taken a hit between the eyes. "That's his name, but if it *was* him, the man we both saw, how could he be in a hospital three hundred miles away and here at the same time?"

"It's impossible."

Lucas sits on the edge of the couch. "It couldn't be! And yet ... Grandpa was the only person she was engaged to. I know he's still alive. I mean, I'll know as soon as he passes through to the other side. It hasn't happened yet."

"How will you know when —"

"Unless ..." He stares straight ahead, lost in his own thoughts.

"Unless what?"

"Eh? Uh, look, I've never been very good at picking up the old man's thoughts. I haven't even known him that long. Somehow he's able to close me off pretty good, but it's possible ... it's possible that he *is* here."

"Oh sure! He's not only alive three hundred miles away, like you said, but he's changed into a young man and traveled here."

"Doc's told me that things like that can happen. If my grandfather's in a deep enough coma, it's possible. He could be astral-traveling. We could be seeing something called a doppelgänger."

"A what?"

"A doppelgänger. It's an exact copy, a double of a person who's still alive, only the doppelgänger isn't flesh and blood, it's a kind of moving picture. It could be Grandpa projecting himself as a young man to a place that's very important to him. I'm still new to all the names they give this stuff, but I think that's what they call it."

"I won't even ask what astral-traveling is, but a doppel-whatever ... can it yell at someone?"

"I don't know. Maybe he was remembering a conversation with her and you just happened to be there. I wish Doc was here."

"Well, all I can say is, I'm sorry he's your grandfather."

"Why?"

"Because he was mean, vicious. He was horrible to me — to her!"

Lucas sighs heavily. "It doesn't sound like him."

"But you said you haven't known him that long."

"Not until Doc arranged for me to live with him. But I like the old guy. He's been kind to me in a distant sort of way. He was always so sad. As if he didn't really live completely in this world, as if there was some inner place ... Maybe that's where I got this from." He jabs his temple with a finger. His laugh is short and dry.

"Do you think maybe your grandpa has it wrong? Perhaps the gardener and Susannah were planning to run away together. They seemed to be together here last night, and she wasn't afraid of him then."

"Or maybe he hadn't given her cause to be afraid yet. Like I said, what we saw was probably a replay of an event that happened a long time ago."

"But her fiance, your grandfather — that young man in the garden — sounded like he was determined to *stop* her from seeing this guy — at any cost."

His voice is stiff. "If the gardener was a creep, maybe Susannah couldn't see it. Maybe she didn't know him like Grandpa did."

"Or maybe your grandpa was jealous. I just don't think the gardener would attack her, okay? I think he loved her. And I think she loved him." I feel my cheeks warm at the memory of the man with the glistening curls. "When I saw her in the mirror it was as if she was talking to someone named Nikos and asking him why he went without her, why he didn't wait for her. And then she saw me."

"She spoke directly to you?"

"Yes. She asked me to find him – Nikos. That's why I'm sure that's the gardener's name. She said she could feel him near her, but she couldn't see him. I bet they *were* going to run away together. And then, somehow, she was killed and her body was buried in the garden. And she wants to know why someone, probably the killer, left her to die."

Lucas stares at me. "What do you mean, buried in the garden? Her grave is right there in the cemetery."

"The vicar that works there now, Reverend Pikeskill, told me he found her bones in the garden behind the storage shed about twenty years ago. *He's* the one who buried her in the cemetery."

Lucas paces back and forth, hands gripped tightly together. "This doesn't make sense. You say she was buried in the soil of the garden? But I see water – not earth."

"Water?" I ask.

"Yes."

"The river? The pond?"

He stares at me. "The pond, I think."

I say, more to myself than to him, "I guess it'd make sense if she refused to run away with the gardener and he got mad, killed her, then took off after burying her behind the shed."

It does make sense — a terrible awful sense.

Lucas nods slowly. "He killed her and then he ran away. But why is he back here looking for her?"

"I don't know! Did you hear him calling in the garden?"

"Yeah, I heard it. He was saying, 'I'm here. I'm here.'"

"So, how come we can see them together in the past, but they can't find each other now? Susannah said, 'Find him for me.' Why? Because she thinks he killed her? She's searching for her murderer?" I rub my cheeks with the palms of my hands. "It's all so ... so hopeless. So confusing. And like you said, if he *did* kill her why is he looking for her now?"

"For forgiveness? Some people believe a murderer always returns to the scene of the crime."

"Even *dead* murderers?"

As gruesome as it is, we both splutter with laughter.

"What if the gardener loved Susannah in a sick sort of way," Lucas says, "and he didn't really mean to kill her. Maybe his guilt is too much to deal with, even in death."

I lean my aching head against the pillows. "Your grandpa's dying. Is that why he's thinking about Susannah now?"

"Yeah. Cancer. He's in a hospice. You know, he really is a nice guy."

"That's not the impression I got when he confronted me — her — in the garden. And if he's not the murderer what does he want with her now?"

Irritation washes over his tired face. "I don't have the answers, okay? Only the questions, just like you. Maybe he's looking to see if she's come back here and if she's forgiven him."

"But what does *he* need forgiveness for?" I say loudly. "And why would he think her spirit would even be looking for him? Especially if he knew she didn't love him. For all he'd know, she could still be alive, with sixteen grandchildren! The old woman Reverend Pikeskill talked to said Jeremy left the area right *after* the gardener and Susannah disappeared. That doesn't match your grandfather's story, does it? *That's* pretty suspicious, don't you think? How do you know he didn't kill her *and* the gardener?"

He bolts to his feet, his face a dark red. "Because I know my grandfather. He's no killer!"

I say nothing, remembering the cold fury in the eyes of the thin man in the garden.

"He – wouldn't – kill – anyone," Lucas says slowly and evenly.

"Okay, okay. Forget it."

He shoves his hands into his pockets and walks back and forth in front of me. "It can't be. Not him. No way."

"I said forget it. Jeez!"

"But, I wonder ..."

"Wonder what?" I ask his legs as they go by for the umpteenth time. "Sit down! You're making me dizzy!"

He crouches in front of me. "There *was* something my grandfather wasn't telling me about Susannah."

I open my mouth, but he holds up one finger and points it at me.

"He would never have hurt her!" he snaps. "That's not it."

"So you said. Fine. Okay! It was probably the gardener. Take it easy." I wait. "So? What *wasn't* your grandfather telling you?"

"When I called him after I got here he was still pretty lucid. I told him I'd found her grave in the cemetery and ..."

"And?" I want to scream at him.

"And he seemed really surprised, okay? Shocked, almost. He kept saying, 'You found her gravestone? In the cemetery?' I asked him if he'd told me everything, and he said I didn't need to know everything. My job was to find out if she was here and if she was all right."

"But she's not all right, is she?" I cry.

"No, but I'll work it out in time. The voices are all around me, but I can't sort them out yet. Right now it's like watching a play – sometimes with only bits of sound and shapes and sometimes only in pantomime. Soon I'll see the whole thing."

"There's one possibility we've avoided talking about," I say.

"What?"

"Her papa was nuts last night. Really crazy. Maybe he's the one who ..."

Lucas nods. "I thought of that, but I don't think he'd actually hurt her."

"You didn't think Jeremy would've either, but I *saw* how mean he was to her. He could have done it. So could her father! I hate them both! They're horrible – trying to get her to do what *they* want. The other one, Nikos, loved her, really loved her. He wouldn't –"

"Listen – it happened a long time ago. I've had to learn to put stuff like this into, uh, perspective."

"Admit it, Lucas, you don't know who killed her. Do you?" I demand.

"No ... no, I don't."

I feel the hairs on the back of my neck lift, remembering the dreadful wrath of the silver-haired papa and the satisfied smile on the face of the dark thin man when he slunk back into the shadows last night. Do I want to be there if they get together with Susannah one last time? No, I don't!

"I want all this to stop," I wail. "Make it all go away!"

"It won't go away, Thea, unless I ... we do something."

"You're telling me we're seeing three ghosts and one doppel-thingy. And we have to sort out who killed Susannah to get any peace and quiet around here," I say sarcastically. "Hey! We'll become detectives! Our witnesses? All dead! It should be a breeze. Why don't we start by talking to your grandfather's doppel-whatever?"

"Doppelgänger. And yes, we're seeing ghosts – although Doc calls them Earth-bound spirits. And yes, they can tell us what happened if we handle them right. But you don't have to stay around if you don't trust me."

Reverend Pikeskill said the air had a thousand voices and I had to trust the right one. Do I take a chance? Should I trust this one?

Chapter Twenty-four

"How did your grandfather know you could come here and get in touch with Susannah?" I ask quietly. "Why do you keep saying you see and hear things?"

His answer is almost a whisper, as if he's running out of energy.

"Because I'm psychic."

"Psychic?"

"A seer, a medium, a clairvoyant, a channeler — whatever you want to call it."

"Like a fortune-teller?"

He smiles sadly. "In a way."

"How did this happen to you?"

"I was born this way. Voices. Sounds. Cries. Shouts. In the air. Out of the walls. All my life. I'd see the people, too. Everywhere. In and out of sight. Coming and going. Trying to talk to me. Even in my sleep. It's like having ten radios and televisions on in your head, picking up all the stations in the world. I didn't talk much as a kid, mostly because I couldn't hear anything clearly from the outside world. I was totally, completely alone. Before my grandfather took me in, I was in a … a special home. Almost six years."

"You mean a hospital?"

He nods. "Kind of. They told my parents I was autistic. Then I met a doctor who thought differently. Doc was the first person I could really hear. It was like he could put his voice on a frequency I could pick up. He took me to different houses and places, and I heard voices in each place – all of them connected to people who'd lived there. When he explained that I was hearing people who were dead, it scared me silly."

I ask, "How could he know you weren't making things up?"

"I gave him names and dates, and Doc checked them out. I was right about ninety-five per cent of the time. Sometimes the facts were confused, but in the end they panned out."

"You hear dead people?"

He nods. "Doc said I was an amazingly gifted psychic. He said my talent made his look like a one-station radio. He taught me how to shut down the part of my mind that hears the voices. But it takes concentration. And when I'm emotionally involved, like now, it's harder and harder to shut down, to get some quiet time. But Doc told me I wasn't crazy. No one had ever said that before."

"Sounds like he saved your life."

"He did. He's great. He doesn't know I'm doing this for Grandpa – he's over in England doing research – and I don't think he'd like it much. I haven't had enough training. But I promised my grandfather. Doc explained to Grandpa about me, you see."

"And your parents?"

He shrugs. "They gave up a long time ago. They'd tried – doctors, drugs, therapists – but no one could help me. I would just stare and not respond to anything most of the time. Other times, I'd lose control. I'd get overloaded with all those voices and lights and colors, and go kind of ballistic – wrecking things, stuff like that. So when I was ten they put me in the home."

"The doctor – Doc – did he try to get in touch with your parents when you started getting better?"

"My parents moved to South America about five years ago – my dad's an engineer. He hadn't talked to my grandfather for years but left Grandpa's name with the home in case of emergency. Doc wanted me out of the hospital but close enough to come for visits, so he called Grandpa first. Grandpa and my parents talked it over and they agreed I'd go and live with him in Treehorn, Saskatchewan. Six months ago he got really sick. When they put him in the hospice about a month ago he asked me if I would come here and listen for Susannah." He smiles. "And here I am. Face it – I'm weird."

"At least you know who you are." I'm trembling, my arms wrapped tightly around my knees.

"You'll be okay, Thea," he says softly.

"Oh yeah? Maybe I'll never be Thea or anybody ever again." Tears burn my eyelids.

"Once we've figured out what's going on here, maybe your memory will come back."

That's what the vicar said. Are they right? I close my eyes and listen to the morning breeze shushing through the vines surrounding the little cottage. A face, dark and intense, flutters past my inner vision. I remember the brush of his lips on mine. The lips of a murderer?

I say quickly, "Aren't you afraid of living in this place? Of Nikos? If you're right, he probably killed someone."

"I'm not afraid of him. Maybe I should be, but I'm not. He can't hurt me."

"How do you know that?" My eyes are burning and I rub them hard.

"I just do — hey, you're falling asleep on your feet. Why don't you go on home? You're all muddy, and your eyes are falling out of your head."

"Gee, thanks." As I stand up to go, panic flutters in my chest. "But Papa and Susannah are in my house. How can I —"

"I'll be close by. I always am. Just call me. I'll hear you."

My smile feels twisted. "With all those other voices getting in the way?"

He looks at his feet. "I can hear yours. It's a clear channel between us — has been ever since I moved here. You don't have to speak. I can hear you, especially when you need help."

"You can read my mind?" I exclaim, horrified.

"No. Only ... it's just that I can sense certain things." His face is flushed.

"So how do I know I'm not picking up all *your* confused thoughts? Maybe *that's* what's happening to me."

"I don't think so."

"Well, do me a favor," I say. "I'm having enough trouble filling this head of mine with my own memories, so I'd appreciate it if you'd stay clear of it!"

With that, I leave the cottage and run through the morning mist toward Susannah's garden.

CHAPTER TWENTY-FIVE

I run until I reach the pond. I feel bad about shouting at Lucas, but I'm too embarrassed to go back. In the distance the early morning sun rests on top of the church steeple, casting long shadows across the garden. It's cool and dim in the circle of bushes that ring the pond. What does that murky pool have to do with Susannah's death? A small mauve moth, spread out on the still black surface, floats past my reflection. A hand reaches over my shoulder and lifts it out of the water.

I look up into Lucas's eyes and say, "It's dead."

He blows gently on the damp wings. They tremble and flutter. "No, it's just broken out of its cocoon." Thin spidery legs stretch and bend on the tip of his finger. He eases the bedraggled creature onto a thick blade of grass hanging over the water.

"He'll just fall in again."

Lucas looks at me sadly. Behind his head, the little moth rises off the blade of grass and flaps slowly toward the sun.

I stare at it in wonderment and shame.

"Why can't you ever leave me alone?" I mutter.

"I'm sorry."

He walks away, shoulders hunched, head down. Oh heck.

"Lucas? Don't be mad. Look, you said you wanted to know more about the spirit you can feel all through the cottage – Nikos, the gardener – right?"

"Yeah."

"Maybe the vicar can help. He knows most of the history around here. He told me about finding Susannah's body – maybe he can find out something about the gardener."

Lucas's face brightens instantly. "Hey, let's go now!"

"The church won't be open yet. I'll get some sleep. You do the same. Come and get me at noon."

He hesitates. "Come? Like knock on the door? Can't we just meet somewhere?"

I stand up, hands on hips. "Don't be silly. Germaine will be the only one there. Besides, I'll be waiting."

He grins and runs one hand over his hair. "Okay. Noon."

With a swish of leaves he's gone.

When I open the back door and step into the kitchen they're *all* there. Staring. Wee demands, "Where you *been?*"

Agatha cries, "Thea! You're covered in mud. What ... I thought you were upstairs asleep."

"I bet she was sleepwalking again," Ellie offers. "Were you?"

Wilton nods slowly. "Is that what happened? Can you, er, remember anything about it? If you're sleepwalking again ... maybe your memory is coming back. Maybe –"

"Sit down," orders Germaine. "Here. It's hard-boiled by now, but you can darn well eat it."

I tap the egg with my spoon. Sleepwalking? Will that cover it? They seem willing enough to believe it.

"I woke up sitting by the pond," I say. "I guess I slipped in the mud or something."

"We'll have to lock her in again after she's asleep," Agatha says. "Like we used to do."

A nameless dread drops over me. The family disappears behind a picture forming in front of my eyes. A door – a dark door. White hands pounding on it and a voice that cries, "Papa! Papa! Please. Let me out!"

Around my head a gray mist grows thicker, closes in on me. It's her. I know she wants to get inside my head.

"NO!" The word shatters the mist into thin trails.

"A curse is on her if she stay," someone whispers.

"Her eyes are funny," another voice says. "Is she having a fit? And what's she mumbling about? A curse?"

"Thea?" Someone shakes me gently by the shoulders.

I look up into Agatha's frightened eyes. Behind her hovers the rest of the Crew.

"Are you okay? Are you going to faint again? Should we take her back to the doctor, Wilton?"

"Maybe we should," he says from my other side.

"I'm okay." I push them away. "When did you have that bed and dresser carried up to the third floor? How long did I stay there? Who let me out? Has that always been my room? When was I *let out*?"

They exchange frightened looks. Am I babbling? Yes. What have I said?

Wilton looks at me closely. "You were never locked in – except to keep you from sleepwalking. And always with your permission. It started only a few weeks before the accident. You were found wandering around the pond at night – on more than one occasion. You make it sound as if you were a prisoner. You weren't. And the furniture has always been there. The church representatives said it was too big and heavy to carry down, so they agreed to leave it there."

"Oh ... then Papa had it moved up there. Of course! He locked me in! I mean *her*. He locked *her* in. That's why I see her there."

"What? See who? Who's Papa?"

"Nothing. Nobody. Just dreams. I'll have a bath and go back to bed. Lucas just said he'd come over later and –" Oops.

"Lucas? Who's Lucas?" Agatha demands. "You *just* left him? Where?"

"He's looking after the Whiteheads' place. He lives –"

"You were *just* with him?" Her eyes are suspicious. "Have you been out with him? All night? And all this talking and meandering is just a smokescreen? Well?"

I shake my head. "A smokescreen? Get serious." I grab a piece of toast and make for the door.

"Don't you march off yet, Thea."

I stop and glare at her.

"Okay, so you were just talking over the fence or whatever. In any case, Ellie has the day off. A teachers' meeting. Which she didn't tell me about until this morning. And Wee always stays home when Ellie does. So I'll expect you to get them fed. If you've been hanging around wasting time with some boy, then you're perfectly capable of –"

"Mama!" Ellie cries. "She's been sleepwalking. That boy, Lucas, hardly knows her. He was talking to her yesterday about how to fix up the garden. Right, Thea? Isn't that what you told me?"

"Thanks, Ellie," I say. "But I was out all night with my *old friend* Lucas." I smile at Agatha. "*Now* are you going to lock me in my room?"

"You see, Wilton? She's even more defiant. Out of control."

"Maybe we should call Dr. Browning," Wilton says.

Agatha rolls her eyes. "Wilton! Please! Listen, Thea, I think you should know that amnesia victims usually don't act like this. I've read every paper I can. They don't usually become secretive. And they certainly don't talk about people who aren't there. I'm almost sure you're deliberately tormenting us. But I don't know why. What's happening to you? You used to be so ... so centered!" The last word ends in a wail.

As I stomp up the stairs chewing on the toast, I wonder what she means? Centered. Huh. I have nothing in my center.

Or do I?

One thing is for sure. I'm gaining some control over Susannah. I refused to let her come into my thoughts down there, and I more or less won. But should I keep fighting her? If I do, how will I find out who killed her?

After a quick shower, I walk into the room where Susannah was kept captive by her father. It's warm — she isn't here. I wrench the window open to let in fresh air, and when I look up I see something I haven't noticed before — spidery writing etched on the windowpane in the top righthand corner. Scarcely daring to breathe, I climb onto the bed and peer closely at it.

Susannah Beatrice Lever, 1929

'She has heard a whisper say,
A curse is on her if she stay.'

I cannot stay. Turn the key
and I will fly
Fly down to Camelot.

I stare at it a long time. Is this part of the poem Lucas quoted? The Lady of ... whatever? *A curse is on her if she stay*. I read it again and again, wretched with misery. She didn't escape. The curse was on her. And the curse was death. Given the chance, who would she have chosen to run away with? Jeremy? Surely not. It had to have been Nikos. But what could have happened to end her hope of happiness with this man she loved so much?

I'll never know. Reality, dreams, past events, they're all the same for poor Thea. My once empty brain is crammed full of jumbled, messy, mixed-up things. Hot tears burn my eyelids. She must have felt so alone. Like me.

I look down to the garden. Near the pond I see Purr – wrapped around the shoulders of my silent guardian, standing under a tall silver willow. Lucas waves. I wave back.

I'm wrong. I'm not alone after all.

Chapter Twenty-six

At exactly noon there's a soft knock on the back door. Germaine makes a halfhearted move toward it, but I wave her away. Lucas stands on the bottom step of the back stoop, flanked by the Two Sisters gazing up at him, openmouthed. For the first time I see how tanned and good-looking he is, with his high cheekbones and slanted eyes, his hair brushed back and falling to his shoulders.

"Where you going?" Wee asks, as I push my way out the door.

"We've got something to do. You can't come."

"You're supposed to look after us," Ellie says.

"You're old enough to watch Wee and you know it."

"But *you're* the one Mama and Daddy say has to look after us. Let us come. Please?"

Wee hangs on to the cuff of my shorts. "Please, please, please, please?"

"We've got to talk to the vicar ..."

"Going to get married?" Ellie giggles.

I stare daggers at her. "You – can't – come."

Lucas clears his throat. The girls wait, gape-jawed, for

him to speak. "If you stay here and play in the yard we could, say, have a picnic. In an hour or so. You could make the food. While we're —"

With a loud whoop they cram through the door, shouting at Germaine.

"It worked!" he says. "It just popped into my head and it worked!"

"So there's more in that brain of yours than voices, huh? Let's go before they change their minds." I can't help grinning at the look of pride and amazement on his face.

Silently we walk along the crushed-stone paths between tall moss-smeared crosses, red marble pillars and round-topped headstones. A few graves, surrounded by their concrete boundaries, have been newly planted with anemic petunias and leggy marigolds.

I move closer to Lucas when we pass the tree that stands over Susannah's grave. I stare at the path and let out a long breath when we reach the corner of the church. The vicar's station wagon is there, but the front door to the building is locked.

"His study's on the other side," I say. "Maybe we can get his attention."

The leaded windows are higher than I realized. Lucas forms his hands into a foot rest and hoists me into the air. Scrabbling and clutching the dirty stones, I reach high and rap my knuckles on one of the little panes of glass. Then I drop down and we stand back. A chubby hand cranks open the window, reaches out and points toward the back of the church. At the top of a short flight of concrete stairs we find a door that opens easily into a short hall.

"Come, come, children." Reverend Pikeskill waves at us from the doorway of his study. "If you hadn't dropped by I'd have had to seek you out today."

"This is Lucas," I say. "He's also interested in Susannah and her father. I've told him about — what I told you."

"How do you do." Reverend Pikeskill looks intently at Lucas. "I believe I've seen you wandering around the churchyard. Come in. You're pale, Thea. Are you well?"

"I'm okay. Just a bit tired."

He beams at us. "I've been doing some research about the Lever family. And I've come up with something quite, *quite* fascinating."

"You've found out more about Susannah?"

"As a matter of fact, yes. Well, I don't know how much good they'll be, but they certainly give some idea about the world she lived in."

He reaches behind him and lifts onto the table an enormous black folder, held together with ribbon ties.

"What's that?"

"People who have passed on can still communicate with us — in very concrete ways. Sometimes things they do in their lives give us clues about who they were and what they've done and —"

"Like what?" I interrupt.

"Well, some people tell us about themselves through letters or journals. And there are other ways, too." He begins to undo the ribbons on the folder. "I asked some of the older church members if they had anything relating to the Levers – letters, anything – and one elder said his father had found this folder after Lever left. He offered it to Reverend Gallagher, but he had no use for the contents, so the fellow hung on to it. I, however, was only too pleased to take it last night."

He opens the folder. A thick layer of tissue lies on top of a pile of yellowing paper. Lucas stands beside me, his shoulder pressing against mine. Reverend Pikeskill lifts the tissue. I suck in a sharp breath.

The garden.

Just like the garden Thea painted over and over, the garden that hangs on the walls of the third-floor bedroom. But this is the formal tended garden of my dreams, painted by a more skilful hand – and signed SBL with an ornamental swirl. Dark blue shadows and vibrant sun splashes, magnificent stands of rosy hollyhocks, blue delphiniums, purple lupins, dazzling speckled tiger lilies and more.

The next painting has been folded over twice and almost covers the desk. On a vapory blue background she's painted an oval frame about an inch wide, dark brown, with little curlicues at the top and a long rounded handle below – like a hand mirror. Where the glass would be is a curious scene. In the exact center is a tree-encrusted island, with a river running around it. A little empty boat floats in the blue-green water.

In the middle of the island just above the trees rise four

gray towers of a castle. At the bottom, surrounded by a froth of trees is a dainty replica of the garden — tiny silver fountain and all. From the top of the mirror's frame a spider's web drifts down and spins itself into a gossamer fabric of intense colors that floats out into the misty blue. Just like the kind I put up in my room.

In a rough whisper Lucas breaks the silence. "'Willows whiten, aspens quiver, little breezes dusk and shiver thro' the wave that runs for ever by the island in the river.'"

"It does have the feeling of that poem, doesn't it?" Reverend Pikeskill says. "So romantic. Poor girl. She must have been a lonely dreamer."

With that he folds the painting and turns the paper over. I gasp when I recognize the strong face with its high-bridged nose and large eyes. Susannah's head is turned slightly, showing an elaborate coil of light brown hair at the nape of her long neck. She's wearing a white lace blouse trimmed with pale green ribbon. At the curve of her breast is a posy of delicate pink flowers.

"It's the painting that used to hang over the mantel in the house," I whisper. I don't tell him that the blouse is the same one Susannah was wearing when she stood in front of the mirror.

"She was really very talented," Reverend Pikeskill says softly. "A beautiful young woman, and there's more in that face — a grave intelligence and a sweetness of soul. No doubt she spent her life trying to please everyone."

"Especially Papa," I say.

It's weird to be looking at a face that's so young yet so serious – and knowing what's ahead for her. Did she know? It's not fair. I have to help her.

Reluctantly, Reverend Pikeskill turns to the next picture. *Papa*. Younger than when I saw him. The face is broad, but not pouchy yet, the silver hair streaked with dark brown. He's actually smiling, a strained twist of his lips, but his eyes have the same spooky blueness I found so unnerving to look into.

"Odd eyes," the vicar says. "Almost gray. With a hint of the madness that assailed him. An arrogant nose. I understand his family was upper class. A man of his times, no doubt – prejudiced, narrow-minded, perhaps. And at times mean-spirited. Yet a hint of passion in that mouth."

My knees shake so hard I have to sit down.

"I can't help but wonder about the next painting," he adds, "perhaps you know him?"

He turns Susannah's father face down and reveals a figure standing with his back to a wide border of white peonies and high black foliage. He's dressed in simple work clothes. In one hand he holds a straw hat and in the other the handle of a long shovel. On the bottom of the page, in ink, the artist has written, "NIKOS, May 23, 1929."

CHAPTER TWENTY-SEVEN

Silence drifts around us with the dust motes and streaks of golden sunlight, yet I feel as if I am standing alone in a cold shadow.

Lucas is staring at the picture with a concentration that's frightening.

Reverend Pikeskill is the first to speak. "*Do* you know who this is?"

I nod. "We were hoping you'd be able to find out about the gardener. This is him."

"The gardener – but how do you know?"

"I just know. How can we find out more about him?"

"Without a last name I don't see how we can," he says, eyeing me uncertainly. "Look, why don't you take these paintings, Thea? They might help. I know you'll take good care of them."

"No! No ... I can't. It could bring her back. I don't want to see her, or him. I –" My throat tightens.

Now the vicar's alarmed. "Has anything happened that you want to tell me about? I'll try to help."

"Thanks, but you can't," says Lucas. "It might be best if

you keep the paintings here for a while, okay?" His face is chalky and his speech choked. "I need time to see ..." Slowly, as if his muscles are melting, he sinks to the floor.

"Lucas!" I kneel down beside him and shake him hard.

Reverend Pikeskill moves me aside. "Give him space to breathe. He's fainted. Does he get enough to eat?"

He turns Lucas onto his side. I realize I'm wringing my hands and letting out little hiccuping sobs.

"We'll just let him be for a few minutes. His pulse is strong. He'll be okay."

"How do you know that?" I demand. "You don't know what he's gone through. He's been in hospital for years and years. His doctor warned him not to get too involved until he'd had more training. Look — he's hardly breathing!"

Reverend Pikeskill stares down at Lucas, a puzzled frown creasing his forehead. He checks his pulse again. "What do you mean, training? Why has he fainted, Thea?"

Tears burn my eyes. "I don't know if he'd let me tell you. Check his pulse again. Please, check it."

"He's okay. Calm down, calm down."

"Don't tell me to calm down," I shout. "Someone killed Susannah. *Killed* her. That's what she told me. And now he's —"

His head swivels sharply. "Susannah Lever spoke to you?"

"Yes. And I've talked to her. It's —"

He clutches the edge of the desk. "You've talked to her?"

"Yes! Yes! How many times do I have to tell you?"

I put one hand on Lucas's shoulder and feel his warmth.

"He sees them, too."

"Both of you?"

"Yes. I'm not kidding, Reverend Pikeskill."

He hastens to say, "I know you're not kidding, Thea — I do believe you. It's just hard to take in. Lucas, he's special, isn't he?"

"Yes. And we've got to sort this mess out. Or else Lucas ... well, he may get lost inside himself again."

And without Lucas I'm not sure I can make it.

Lucas groans softly and rolls over onto his back. We help him sit up.

"Sorry," he mutters. "This used to happen a lot. I — I didn't expect ... Anyway, there was a lot going on in there suddenly." He points to his head and gives a sickly grin. Color slowly returns to his face.

After a glass of water he insists he's okay, but Reverend Pikeskill makes him sit down in one of the leather chairs.

"Thea's told me that you and she have seen Susannah."

Lucas gets a hunted expression in his eyes.

"Don't worry," the vicar says quickly. "I won't interfere in any way. Even so, could you tell me a bit about what's happening — only if you want to, that is."

"It wouldn't help. There's nothing you can do. I just have to be careful." Lucas glances at me. "We'll sort it out."

Something in me snaps. "Will we? How? How can we get rid of them? I want Susannah and her father and that Nikos and your grandfather's doppelgänger to go away. I want them to leave me alone!" I brush away angry tears.

"Now, now, Thea," Reverend Pikeskill murmurs. "What do you mean by doppelgänger? How is Lucas's grandfather involved?"

I turn on him. "What difference does it make? What good are you? You probably don't even believe us. You'll probably call some social worker the second we leave."

Reverend Pikeskill shakes his head sadly and hands me a big starched handkerchief. "No, no, I won't. I promise. And you're quite right, I'm not much good, but I do believe everything you say. All I will offer is my faith and my confidence. I'm sorry I can't do more."

"Me, too," Lucas murmurs, as I snuffle into the handkerchief. "I only meant –"

"It doesn't matter," I mumble. "Let's just go, okay? We promised Wee and Ellie."

We all walk to the back door.

"Never forget – I'm here if you need me," the vicar says, his pleasant round face crumpled with concern. "Are you sure you'll be all right?"

Lucas nods. "I'll let you know when you can help. Just keep the paintings, okay?"

I add, "I'm sorry I yelled at you."

Reverend Pikeskill smiles. "Don't give it another thought, Thea. Righteous passion cleanses the soul. Just be very, very careful."

After more assurances that we are to call any time for anything he closes the door with a quiet click.

This time, we make a wide circle around Susannah's

grave, and I grip Lucas's arm tightly.

"Are you okay?" he asks.

"I think so. You?"

His voice is edgy. "Yeah."

"Did you get some sleep?"

"A bit. Not much." His face is still pasty and he's avoiding my eyes.

"Are you mad at me for yelling?"

"Huh? Heck no."

"Was there something you saw in those paintings? Something I should know about?"

He looks across the cemetery toward the river. "No, it's ... I just have to check something out first. Can we forget everything for a while? I've put a lid on all this – for as long as it'll last – and I'd like to – to take a break."

Take a break? From me. Disappointment squeezes my chest. I'm going to be on my own again.

I'm about to duck through the gap in the hedge when he grabs my hand. A tingle of electricity goes up my arm.

"I know this is lousy for you, Thea. I told you I watched you for almost two weeks before your accident. You were really unhappy."

"I was? You could tell what she – what I was feeling?"

"Sad. Lonely. And angry. Mostly at your parents. Unsettled. It was like you were suffocating at times, and at other times you were frightened and worried. Sometimes you'd sit outside and paint. Sometimes you'd stand by this hedge and stare out over the river as if the whole world was on the other side and you'd never get to see it. Even with your family around you were always alone. But you seemed so proud and so solitary that I didn't ... I couldn't approach you."

For a split second I see myself sitting in a secret corner of the garden, hiding, my chest crushed with anger, frustration, hurt. Someone calls my name. I don't answer. I want to be left alone forever. I want never to be left alone again.

Warm fingers grip my hand. "You'll be okay. You've got to believe me. Solving Susannah's problem will solve yours."

I shrug. "Dr. Browning figured Thea's family would make me better. But they haven't. Now *you* say Susannah will solve my problem."

"I didn't say Susannah herself would. By helping her, you help Thea."

I smile at him. "Thea? You mean me?"

He touches my forehead with a fingertip. His eyes are so close I can see tiny flecks of gold in the green. "Yeah. You."

I feel a warm flush creep up my face. I tense, remembering the way I felt in the cottage when the dark-eyed Nikos leaned close and kissed me ... Susannah. Is it Susannah who's feeling this tingling excitement at Lucas's closeness? No, it's me. Thea!

Suddenly I feel light and happy. "Yeah," I say. "Me."

Lucas laughs and pushes me toward the gap in the hedge. "Come on. We've got a picnic to go to."

Chapter Twenty-eight

Dandelions scatter like tiny sun dots through the grass, and birds chirp and squeak from every bush and tree. It's hard to believe that anything could possibly be wrong in this sunny garden. There are no lost memories. No ghosts. No strange dark men in the shadows.

A small figure stands up under one of the apple trees and waves madly. "We here. We ready!"

An old plaid blanket has been spread under the gnarled branches and scattered with old embroidered pillows. Smack in the middle are a plate of sandwiches, a big jug of something pink, and chocolate brownies still in their tin pan and covered with frost.

"Come. Sit. Eat," Wee says, importantly.

"We made peanut butter — some with strawberry jam and some with bananas. And Germaine made cream cheese and pickles. She's gone home early," says Ellie, pouring some of the pink stuff into a plastic tumbler and handing it up to Lucas. "You can sit down, you know. We're not going to eat *you*."

Wee giggles dramatically into her hand, her eyes

scrunched up. "We no eat you!"

Lucas slides down cross-legged on the edge of the blanket and eyes them as if they're an unknown species of bodiless spirits.

"You no like us?" Wee asks, with a worried frown.

"Oh, no. I like you. I ... well, I've read about them, but I've never been on a picnic before."

Amazement brightens their faces.

"Never?" Ellie asks. "Thea always used to make picnics for us. We had them by the pond. But last year –" she turns to me "– you said you didn't like it there anymore."

I slowly chew the crust of my sandwich, remembering my recent meeting with Jeremy Fitzgerald. Why would Thea – I – suddenly become reluctant to go near that spot? Had I met him there – before the accident? Is that why the picnics stopped? But the pond is quickly forgotten when Ellie suggests we play I Spy.

Before long even Lucas is laughing, explaining to Wee that you can't spy an ant and still claim victory when it disappears underground. I laugh, too, and then yawn loudly.

Ellie pokes me. "Not enough sleep, huh?"

I see a gleam of the old Ellie in her sharp eyes, but I ignore it. Instead I yawn again and nod. Everyone else yawns. When we're through laughing we all flop down with pillows under our heads. Lucas's back is to me. I want to touch the curve of his spine, reassure myself that he is there, that I can sleep. He turns over and looks at me. "I won't go anywhere."

I don't know how long I've slept, but when I open my eyes again I am tense and alert. The sky is still blue and the blossoms still hang above my head, but the birds are silent — and the stillness is thick and ominous. Lucas is sitting up, staring toward the back of the garden.

Someone is standing in front of the pond. His black curls glisten and the white of his shirt is blurred, as if white paint has touched watery paper.

He holds the long-handled shovel he had in the painting. In fact, it is the painting come to life. He knows we're here. Suddenly, he beckons with a sweep of his straw hat, turns and walks through eye-shattering light toward the dark garden behind him.

"Lucas?" I whisper.

"It can't be ..." he says faintly.

He reaches out behind him. His fingers are icy cold. We leave the still sleeping girls, and hand in hand slowly follow the dark-haired man — Nikos — toward the cottage. If he murdered Susannah, what does he want with us?

CHAPTER TWENTY-NINE

"He's going to the woods!" I whisper frantically.

"I know. Be quiet. Let me reach him," Lucas says.

"Can you feel Susannah?" I ask.

"No. Can you?"

"Nothing. Lucas, he's gone!"

"No. Look."

A gleam of broken light cuts through the shadowy shapes of the tree trunks. When we edge our way around a huge oak, Nikos is waiting in a small clearing.

"What are you doing here?" Lucas demands. I'm surprised to hear anger in his voice. "Why now?"

Susannah caught Nikos's face perfectly in her painting, but not this potent sadness. The awful stillness surrounding him is like waiting for a clap of thunder to break over our heads. Then from quite near, a voice drifts through the woods, and I realize, with a sickening lurch, that it's coming from him.

"All this time I've been waiting. I came back more than once but couldn't find her. *You* can find her. Tell her I'm finally here. Tell her it's time." He raises the shovel and drives it into the earth. Metal hits stone. Sparks fly. The trees above us swirl as if a giant's hand is stirring them. Loud voices. Shouts of anger. Then, from out of nowhere, a dark shape swoops past us and, like an enormous cape, winds itself around Nikos.

He's gone.

Lucas's face is gray and solid, like one of the statues in the cemetery. I follow him as he creeps to the spot where Nikos stood. There's a fresh cut the width of a shovel deep in the earth.

"Why did he lead us here? What does he want?" I ask.

Lucas pivots on his heel and runs toward the cottage.

"Lucas! Wait!" I am terrified that the black shadow will swallow me up, too.

He's sitting in front of the fireplace, his head in his arms. Breathless, I crouch beside him.

"Lucas?"

"I'm okay," comes his muffled voice. "My grandfather ..."

I grip his shoulder. "What? Has he — ?"

"He's going to the other side. Any time now. I'm sure of it. And he's ..."

After all these years Jeremy Fitzgerald is about to die. What then? Will he cause even more problems?

Lucas nods as if he's read my thoughts. "I think he ... We've got to go back to the woods. It *can't* be the way I see it! We've got to get rid of the girls, then go back there and dig."

"Dig? Where Nikos marked the soil? Do you think he

buried something there before he ran away?"

Lucas's eyes are dazed with misery. "He ... I think he might have before he ... ran away. And I've got to call the hospice in Saskatchewan and find out —"

"Okay, but let's check on the girls first — I don't want them coming here. Then you can phone and we'll come back and dig."

I lead him back through the hedge. He walks like a robot, his face stiff, his eyes unfocused.

"Where you been?" Wee demands.

"Yeah, what have you two been up to?" Ellie's teasing fades when she sees Lucas's face. "What's wrong?"

He lowers himself carefully onto the blanket.

"Yoo-hoo!" someone calls.

I groan. "Oh no. Not Wilton. Not now!"

"Don't you look rather cozy and, uh, Victorian," he says, walking toward us. "Rather like the wonderful picnics of my youth. My grandparents were picnic aficionados. They —"

"What do you want?" I ask. "Aren't you supposed to be working?"

Wilton looks hurt. "Well, yes, but your mother and I have been doing some, uh, serious dialoguing, and we've decided to have a what-do-you-call-it ... family meeting and get input from all of you. So we both got someone to cover for us and, well, here we are. Ready to conference, as Agatha says. We should have done this years ago of course, but Thea —" He stares at Lucas. "I'm sorry, I don't think we've met."

Agatha lumbers across the grass. "You're the summer caretaker next door, aren't you? You've done a great job with their lawns. Perhaps you'd like to earn some extra cash?"

Lucas nods.

"You could cut our lawn once a week?"

He nods again.

Agatha's trying to be pleasant, but Lucas isn't exactly helping. Her feet are puffy, pushing out between the leather thongs of her sandals like pale cushions, and she's sweating heavily.

For a split second I put myself in her place and realize how hard it must be to be pregnant in this heat. Especially at her age. She turns to me. "I'd like you to come inside, please. And the girls, too. We're going to have a talk."

"I can't. I've got things to do. Lucas and I are —"

Wilton's voice is firm. "Lucas will excuse us, I'm sure. And I think you *will* come. You've got away with saying and doing just ... uh, well, just about anything you want since you've been home. We're reaching out for some solutions. The least you can do is come inside and help sort things out."

Embarrassment makes my ears hot.

Lucas stands up. "I better get going. I've got a phone call to make and ... other stuff."

I hiss, "Don't go near that spot without me, okay?"

"I don't intend to. See you later."

He swings up into the apple tree, climbs along a straight

branch and drops out of sight behind the hedge.

"Strange boy," mutters Agatha.

"He is not!" I shout. "He's the nicest person I've ever met."

Wee nods. "Nicest."

"And just about the cutest," Ellie says with a secret smile.

For the first time since I've been home, Agatha laughs. "He certainly is cute, I'll give him that. And if you like him it puts my mind a little more at ease. He does seem quite nice, even if he isn't very chatty."

"Puts your mind at ease?" I ask. "Why?"

Agatha shrugs.

Wilton says, "She and I were worried that he might ... take advantage of your, uh, vulnerable state, so to speak."

"My mindless state, you mean." I'm determined not to give in.

Agatha sighs. "Look, do you think we could talk? I'd like to make things better between us."

This I've got to see. I follow the Crew into the house. If nothing else it will be good for a laugh. And I could do with a laugh right about now.

CHAPTER THIRTY

"You mean you're going to stay home after the baby is born? And you're definitely not going to England?" I ask, searching for the trap in this news.

Agatha pulls a loose thread on one of her shirt buttons. "I won't be staying home for *good*. Just for the summer and a little into September. I've arranged for a colleague to take over. I was going to try for England this month, instead of after the baby was born, but my midwife has refused to let me go. She says my blood pressure is touchy."

"The midwife won't let you go." My voice is harsh. "I see."

"I just finished saying we think that your ... criticisms have some validity."

Wilton picks up. "We do acknowledge that we've been caught up rather too much in our own careers and concerns. Germaine is not someone who goes beyond her paid tasks. We've neglected our duties. We admit it."

I snort. "*Duties*. That's us, right?"

Ellie and Wee sit on a couch, wide-eyed and very quiet, knowing their fate is tied up in the three people facing off across the living room.

"That is most unfair," Wilton says.

Agatha sighs. "I know you've been through a lot, Thea. In time we'll get back to the way things were before the accident. They weren't too bad, were they?"

"All *I* remember is being unhappy."

"You remember?" they say together.

"Not details. Feelings. And everyone tells me I was miserable – Ellie, even Germaine."

There's a stiff moment of silence, broken by Agatha. "Trust Germaine to get in her two cents' worth."

Wilton looks bewildered. "Were you really so unhappy, Thea?"

Agatha adds, "Perhaps we did put more *visible* effort into our work but, Thea, we did care – *do* care – about you and about Wee and Ellie."

"You *care*, huh? You call these past few days caring?"

"Yes! No! I mean, I ... we're trying. You have to realize, Thea, university jobs are hard to come by, and you can't just take time off without jeopardizing your position. And there's preparing lectures and group work and research –"

"How many excuses do you have, I wonder?" I cross my arms.

"Now, Thea," Wilton says, "that's going to get us, uh, nowhere, is it?"

"Let's get down to your plans." I try not to sneer. "So what happens after September?"

"We ... don't know yet. But we'll do something, won't we, Aggie? We'll put a bid in for the house – we have bonds to help out. But we won't be able to stop working if we're going to buy it."

I can feel my lip curl. "So what will change? Except that with a new baby around you'll have even less time for *them*." I point to the dejected pair on the couch.

"You must trust us," Agatha says, her eyes searching my face. "I promise we'll work toward a fairer system."

"Including getting meals and buying food and stuff like that?"

"Your dad and you and I can take turns. Ellie can do simple meals. Maybe we can all prepare a number of things on Sundays and reheat them through the week."

"But I'll have to come right home from school and look after the kids and the baby, right?"

"We've discussed that, too," she says. "We might be able to hire a nanny, maybe one of the women from the shelter. You'll have time for after-school events, for friends. We promise."

"And your groups and classes and that Samaritan business?"

"We'll slowly reduce our hours, but we can't drop everything. This is who we are, Thea. We like our work. But we'll strive to organize our time better. And to seal this promise," she says brightly, looking at Wee and Ellie, "we're taking you all out for dinner. Right now."

"I – I can't go," I say.

"Why not?" Agatha asks.

"Where are we going?" Ellie demands. "Can I wear my red dress?"

"Yes. Of course you can."

"Me wear?" Wee asks.

Ellie offers, "How about my yellow gingham skirt and blouse?"

"Yees!" squeals Wee. "Oh, yes!"

"Thea, why can't you come?" Wilton asks.

The girls crowd around me and beg. Before Wee pulls my arm off I give in. "But we won't be late, will we?"

"She's gotta see lover boy," Ellie says.

Agatha frowns.

"Ellie, shut up!" I snap. "I've been cleaning out the flower beds. We're going to plan the garden, that's all."

"That would be nice." Agatha's face clears. "Okay, you've all got fifteen minutes to get ready. I'll help Wee wash."

As I climb the stairs to find something to wear, I can't help but think that this gooey family togetherness has a time limit. As soon as that baby is born Thea will be back to washing faces and making sloppy macaroni. Unless I take off – maybe with Lucas. A blush creeps up my face and I run up the rest of the stairs.

Half an hour later, we're crowded into Agatha's car on the way to the Golden Carrot. Ellie's hair is a wild bush. The red dress has a tear under one arm, and her sandals are held together with safety pins. Wee sits on my lap, smelling strongly of cheap perfume and soap. Even her nails are clean. The cotton skirt is down to her ankles, but she's so proud of it I can't laugh. With luck, we'll be the only ones in the restaurant, and I won't have to hide behind a menu. The Chalmers-Goodall Family rattles across the city in a rusting heap of a car, brushed and scrubbed for their big night out.

CHAPTER THIRTY-ONE

We arrive home about eight o'clock, full of bean sprouts and shredded carrots. The sun melts like warm honey behind the treetops, and the air is dull, gentle and sweaty.

"I'm going out for a while, okay?" I say to Agatha as we walk up the path.

"Sure, I guess. And thank you, Thea, for asking permission."

I stiffen. "I just wanted to make sure Wee wouldn't be left alone."

"I have to work, but she can play in my office."

Wee is struggling with a tilted ice-cream cone. Yellow cream and chocolate sprinkles ooze down her sleeve.

"See you later, kiddo."

I leave them to deal with the soggy cone and walk to Lucas's cottage. Isn't this what I wanted? To come and go as I please? To finally get rid of the kid? Yet the tightening in my chest at the loving look Wee gave Agatha came as a surprise. Maybe one day I'll figure out exactly what I want. Starting with a decent brain. As I near the cottage my urgency to see Lucas grows. That's something I *know* I want.

The door of the cottage won't open. I rattle the handle and bang my shoulder against the heavy wood.

"Lucas?" I call. "Open up. It's me."

The only answer is the rustle of leaves as a breeze flutters through the vine. I push aside the thick growth over the window, expecting to see Lucas sitting in front of the little fireplace.

The room is empty.

The rack that held his few bits of clothing is empty, too. Even his blue hat is gone. Dread makes my heart turn cold and dense in my chest.

He's left. Gone.

As I stare at the stillness inside trying to understand, a dark shadow zigzags across the windowpanes and passes over the leaves beside me with a deep sigh.

I turn to run, but I'm too late.

A man stands at the corner of the house. His gray suit blends into the shadows, but the gaunt face stands out like a 3-D picture. Red-rimmed eyes flick toward me, then toward the path into the woods.

"Jeremy," I whisper, and he is gone, leaving a faint light, like a crimson blur.

Why is he here? Has he died in that hospice? What was he trying to tell me? Why did he look toward the woods?

I walk down the path, but when I reach the clearing there's no one there, nothing, just the bite of Nikos's shovel in the ground.

I stand for a long time, unable to think of anything but Lucas's betrayal. He said that he would help me, that he wouldn't go anywhere. He's broken his promise.

The moon soars like a newly polished coin above the top of the oak tree. A thick silence fills the clearing. The smells of earth and weedy water surround me and I can feel myself slowly dissolve ... into dust and ashes floating in the air above.

"Lucas!" a deep voice echoes through the open space. "Where are you?"

With a gasp of terror, I come back to earth and scurry through the woods, past the cottage toward safety — toward living breathing people. My family.

CHAPTER THIRTY-TWO

In the old dining room Agatha looks up from her work. Wee is perched at a small table, crayons spread around her. It's a peaceful scene, but I can't join it. I don't seem to belong here.

"Are you okay, Thea?" Agatha asks, pressing one hand into the small of her back. Before I can answer she continues, "I think it's Wee's bedtime. I've been having these funny pains for about an hour. Do you think you could ..."

Five minutes with the kid and she's already palming her off on me. "Wilton's run off, has he?"

"No. He's helping Ellie with her lines for the play. Never mind. I'll handle Wee. I just thought —"

"Well, as long as we're playing Happy Families," I sneer, "why *don't* you do it? By tomorrow it'll be my job again, anyway. Right?"

Wee's voice follows me down the hall. "Thea sad again. I go with her!"

"Leave her, honey," comes Agatha's tired voice. "She needs some space — to be alone."

I snort. Space? To be alone? How much more alone can I be? Lucas is gone. I hate him! I hate Thea and her stupid make-believe. And I hate Susannah and her stupid garden.

I tear the paintings off the wall as I run up to the third floor. "I won't let you in, Susannah! I won't! Stay away from me. Stay away!"

I bang open my bedroom door, and when I start to rip at the garden on the walls a loud crash stops me dead.

The painting table is lying on its side, paper and supplies scattered through a puddle of murky water. I stand mesmerized as a tube of paint lifts into the air. Others follow and hurl across the room, just missing me.

The tall wardrobe doors bang open and shut, paintbrushes splatter dirty water onto the walls, the dresser shakes — its drawers edging open with each thump. A pot of eye shadow skids past my ear, followed by a long silvery necklace. Soon the air is filled with missiles that never quite hit me.

"Cut it out!" I scream. "Stop it! Right now!"

And it does. A silk scarf, jars of makeup, sheets of watercolor paper, and jewelry, suspended in mid-air, fall to the floor. Tinkle. Clank. Flutter. Clack.

I stand in the wreckage, horrified.

"Where is he?" a voice demands.

In a high squeak I ask, "Susannah?"

There's a faint outline of long rippling hair and a white blouse, but the voice is hard and clear. "Where is he?"

"Do you mean Lucas? I don't know. He —"

"You said you'd find him. I know he is close by." Her voice thickens, full of angry tears. "Where is he? He promised he'd never leave me. He said he'd rather die. Why did he leave me?"

The jewelry and papers begin to stir again, rattling along the floor and banging into the baseboards.

"I don't know!" I stamp my foot. "I don't know why people leave! Who do *you* mean? Your papa? Jeremy? Nikos? Did he kill you?" I am shouting now. *"Who are you talking about?"*

"Why did he lie to me? Find him. Find him." Sobbing fills the room. It fills my head.

"Listen to me!" I shout.

The fluttery figure straightens and for a moment Susannah's features are clear and alive, and I know she's listening.

"You have got to tell me *what happened* to you. Show me. Can you do that?"

She's fading fast.

"Can you?" I plead. "Can you?"

Her lips are moving.

"I can't hear you!" I cry.

As she disappears, the things on the floor lift and rattle and then settle with a sigh that swirls around the room.

CHAPTER THIRTY-THREE

The door of my room bangs open. Before I can faint with shock Ellie screeches, "It's Mama. She's really sick! Daddy says it's the baby. It's coming, but it's too soon. Hurry up!"

In The Parents' bedroom, everything's in an uproar. Wee is standing at the foot of the bed crying loudly.

"Hush, Wee," Wilton says. "Now, Aggie —"

"I will not have the hospital called, Wilton," Agatha moans. "Call Jenny." She's lying on her side, her face the color of dough.

"Who's Jenny?" I ask.

Wilton stutters, "The m-midwife. But this is different than the other pregnancies. It's weeks too early. Aggie, I th-think it might be — no *would* be advisable to have a, uh, doctor in on this."

"Call Jenny, damn it! She'll know what to do," Agatha groans. "I'll do whatever she says. Just call!"

Wilton dials the bedside phone with shaking fingers. After he takes forever to describe what's happening the receiver squawks loud enough for all of us to hear it, even above Wee's noise.

"Jenny says doctor, ambulance, hospital – in that order," he announces. Agatha nods miserably, her eyes glazed with pain.

He makes two more phone calls while we crowd around. Wee has lost her pajama bottoms and diaper somewhere along the way.

He hangs up again. "It appears that Aggie will, uh, be transported in the ambulance. I'll follow in my car. You're okay with the girls, Thea?"

Through my teeth I say, "Just get her things together. Hurry up!"

He nods. "Wee and Ellie. You listen to Thea. And it might be a good idea to stay out of the way of the, uh, what do you call them ... ambulance attendants. Perhaps the kitchen for a hot drink? Now, Wee, enough howling. You're upsetting Aggie."

I usher the silent girls down into the kitchen and heat some milk. As I stare into its skimmy bubbles it hits me – what if Aggie dies?

What do I feel for her? Or the new baby? What *should* I feel? At the moment I'm not aware of anything except a curious excitement about the drama going on in The Parents' room above – and on the third floor where a different drama plays out, an angry young woman searching for her murderer.

Madness. All madness. I pour the steaming milk into mugs and order the girls to drink up. They stare at me with frightened eyes. Do my eyes have the same look?

Just then the ambulance wails down our street.

"Amb'lance here," Wee whispers.

"We know that, you little twerp!" Ellie hisses, then asks me. "Should we open the door? Help them?"

"You stay here. I'll go."

"But –"

"Stay here. You don't want to get in the way and slow things down, do you?" Both heads shake vigorously.

The ambulance men are quick and efficient. It brings back the memory of strong brown arms that carried me from the cemetery. Wilton follows the stretcher down the stairs, wringing his hands and muttering, "Watch that corner. And there. Good. Good. Now turn ..." The men ignore him, taking the turns expertly.

As the stretcher slides past me, Agatha's hand reaches out and grabs my arm. I trot alongside.

"Don't look so worried," she says, a faint smile creasing her swollen face. "I'll be fine."

She looks terrible. Shame swells in my chest.

"I'll take good care of the girls," I say, because I can't think of anything else.

"I know you will," she replies, releasing my arm as they carry her through the front door. "I've never doubted your abilities, Thea. Never. Just took advantage of them."

She's gone.

Wilton pats my shoulder. "I'll call as soon as I have news."

When the door clicks shut behind him I stand in the

emptiness of the hall.

And I remember.

I remember a tall brown-and-silver-haired woman in a baggy skirt and sweater standing in that same hallway, handing me a cardboard box packed with shiny tubes of watercolors, unsharpened pencils, boxes of pastels and a handful of green-handled brushes wrapped with a rubber band.

I remember … Agatha lifted the box into my arms and I staggered under its weight, laughing.

"There," she said. "Now you can become the next Emily Carr. Can't have talent like that without tools to develop the craft."

Agatha bought all those paints and supplies. Just for Thea. For me. So I could paint the garden.

Hugging this fragile new memory close, I go back to my sisters.

CHAPTER THIRTY-FOUR

That memory seems to have started something off. While I'm feeding the girls peanut-butter sandwiches, I turn to Ellie. "I didn't put grape jelly on yours."

Her eyes narrow to slits. "Why not?"

"Because you hate grape jelly."

"What else do I hate to eat?"

"Liver. Like me – I hate it, too. And ... let me think ... yeah, peas. You hate peas. But I love them."

"That's right." Her voice is awestruck. "You remember!"

I sit, sandwich halfway to my mouth, while little sparkly lights flash in my head.

"What else?" she demands.

I think hard. My mind is blank. "Nothing. Nothing else."

"Never mind. I bet when you don't try it'll come back. Like trying to remember how a word is spelled. Sometimes you have to get a pencil and let it write itself. Try *not* to remember, like."

I tell her I'll *try* not to try, even though I don't really believe it'll help. But while I'm getting Wee ready for bed I call across to Ellie's room, "Where are those pink-striped pj's of Wee's? They're cooler than these flannel ones."

"I don't know!" Ellie shouts back. "I can't find my own."

"Under bed," says Wee. "I see them one day."

And there they are, covered in dust. No one has noticed that I remembered these pajamas. But I do.

Thea's memories are coming back.

CHAPTER THIRTY-FIVE

Wilton calls about midnight. "How are the girls?"

"I finally got them to bed," I reply. "Is Agatha okay?"

"So far so good, Thea. She has something called pre-eclampsia. Jenny warned her last week to go to the doctor, but Aggie said she didn't have time. Her blood pressure is all over the place. They've given her something to stop the onset of labor and keep the blood pressure under control."

"But will she be okay?"

"She seems, uh, stable, but it's ... serious."

My heart tightens. "The baby. What about the baby?"

"The heartbeat is still strong. There may have to be an operation. But they don't know yet."

"When will she – they – come home?"

"If they can get Aggie and the baby stabilized she may be able to come home in about a week. Unless she goes into labor. If she comes home still pregnant, the doctor says no midwife. Aggie's already arguing with him. I'll stay a while longer. You get some sleep. Lock up before you go to bed."

I wander to the back door and stare out into the night. Let them both be okay. Please, please. I promise to look after the baby. Just let them be okay.

It's quiet outside except for the rumble of far-off traffic. I step out onto the back stoop. Purr glides around my legs, then drops down one step at a time, looking back to see if I'm following.

Everything's falling apart – Agatha in the hospital, Susannah here, Lucas gone.

Where is he? Has he disappeared for good? Or is he just visiting his grandfather? Is old Jeremy Fitzgerald dead? Did he really love Susannah? Maybe that's why Lucas left – to go and get some answers. But if the old man is in a coma …

Leaf shadows swish across the wide expanse of lawn. In the moonlit patches Purr's silvery fur shimmers ahead of me. When we get to the pond he prowls into the dark undergrowth and I sit down on the wide stone seat beside the water.

"Susannah," I whisper, "please help me. Show me what happened."

"So, Susie, here you are," a voice says almost immediately. "I wait by the cypress, but you don't come."

As if my limbs are being pulled by invisible strings I lean forward and grasp the hand that appears in front of me.

"Nikos, I'm so sorry," I hear myself say. "I had to sneak out right after dinner. This was the best place to hide. Papa is having one of his spells. Because of last night he had my furniture moved into the attic and ordered me to stay in the house. Or else he'll lock me in that room! He scares me. He sits in the dark study, muttering about how I am doomed and how he will be punished for being a bad father."

"And now? He does not follow you here?"

"No. I told him that I had a headache and that I was early to bed. I put a double dose of medicine in the tea that Annie took in to him. It will put him to sleep for the night. He never leaves his chair when he's like this. Nikos, I feel so guilty for causing this bout of illness."

"It is not your fault. You have been a good daughter, Susie." Nikos's voice is deep with emotion. "But he was so violent. I am afraid for you. He is a madman. We must decide tonight."

"Yes," I say. "Tonight."

"Young Fitzgerald. We have to be careful around him. He is your papa's spy. He has threatened me."

"Threatened you? How?"

"He says he will go to the police and tell them that I attacked you."

"He wouldn't! I'll deny it. He is just trying to scare you away!"

"Do not worry. I am able to take care of myself. It is you I worry for. He is so jealous. He has a right to be. I take your love away."

I grip Nikos's hand tighter. "I never cared about him. Never! He is as bad as Papa. I've told him I cannot marry him, but he insists Papa will see to it. Jeremy is so superior, so disdainful. I thought he would be glad to end this farce after Papa found ... you and me, but he is determined the marriage will go forward. He claims he cannot live without me."

Heavy warm arms gather me in. I can hear Nikos's heart beat in time with my own.

"I understand his pain. He does love you in his way. Perhaps too much – because he doesn't think of you, just himself and his need for you."

"What will we do? He frightens me as much as Papa does."

"It must be tonight," Nikos says. "I cannot risk him going to the police – they could make things terrible for you. He has said he will accuse me of stealing from him if you refuse to speak against me –"

"No!" I insist. "It won't happen. We'll go tonight. I'll pack and –"

"Do not bring a large bag. We cannot risk showing any hint that you are leaving. I will tell Fitzgerald that I have given up and that I will go. You and I will meet here at eleven o'clock. Come dressed for train travel. Bring one small bag. Nothing more."

"Money? I can't get any –"

"Money does not matter!" he protests.

I hold him tightly. I am not afraid. I will go with him.

"I'll leave a note for Papa. Despite everything, he does love me and I wouldn't want him to worry –"

Abruptly Nikos pushes me away. "I cannot do this. You are giving up too much. You are too young. I am selfish. I am no better than Fitzgerald."

"Don't talk like that. I am choosing to go, Nikos. I'm

dying here. Suffocating. I must go." A terrible thought overwhelms me. "You won't leave without me? You aren't thinking I'm too much of a burden?"

He holds me by the shoulders and looks into my eyes. "I only want what is best for you, Susie."

"Yes. And that is why I am coming with you."

"I will wait for you. I won't leave without you. Now go quickly. Be careful."

He releases me and disappears into the shadows. I run across the lawn, my feet barely touching the ground. I am sure that if I leaped into the air I would float above my garden. I stop for a moment. That is the only sad thing – I will have to leave my garden. But Nikos and I will make our own, around our very own little house. My feet skim up the back stairs. I reach for the handle, but the door is flung open. Before I can call out for Nikos, Papa drags me into the house.

CHAPTER THIRTY-SIX

The kitchen lights are on and the remains of the girls' sandwiches and milk are still littered across the table. I must have fallen asleep on the stone seat. But how did I end up back in the house? Sleepwalking?

If this really happened all those years ago, what will happen next? A horrible thought slams into my head. Did Susannah's papa go completely mad that night? Did he kill her? His own child? On shaking legs I lock up but leave all the lights on. I creep upstairs. The girls are sound asleep.

I lie under my comforter in the dark, fully clothed. Is there more to come? I don't want to see what happened to Susannah – not if her father killed her.

Suddenly, the room turns deathly cold. I burrow my face deep into my pillow, too afraid to reach up and turn on the light. Although I try to deaden them, every one of my senses is on the alert.

Footsteps? Pacing back and forth beside the bed? Suddenly, someone bangs loudly on the bedroom door. Instinctively I sit up, but before I can call out, someone in the room speaks.

"Annie, I know you're out there. You open this door at once! You're supposed to be my friend."

More banging follows – on the inside of the door.

A muffled wail comes through from the hall. "Please don't make such a racket, Miss Susannah. I'd like to help you, but the master has forbidden it. I don't know what to do, and that's a fact!"

"Annie. Let me out. Please. I must go. Please."

"But I'll lose my job, miss. Besides, I don't know where the key is. Honest, miss," the girl whines.

"It's in his desk. I told you. Just get it. You say he's gone to bed. Go to the study and get it."

"What if he woke up and found me there? Oh, I couldn't, miss."

"You must, Annie, you must!"

"I can't. Don't ask me, miss." The girl is crying loudly now. Footsteps quickly run away down the short hall.

"Don't you dare leave me here, Annie! Get the key! Annie!"

Silence thrums through the room. I turn on the light. The room is empty. I flop back onto the pillow. I hug myself into a tight ball and burst into fierce hot tears.

CHAPTER THIRTY-SEVEN

The room is dark when I wake up again. I know I didn't turn off the light. Something rustles nearby. My eyes strain into the muzzy shadows, my ears alert. Another faint rustle and then the scrape of something – a key in the lock? I sit up. A sliver of light and then the door creeps open and a small girl with frizzy yellow hair peers into the room, a candle in one hand.

"Miss? Miss?" she whispers.

"Annie?" Into the faint glow of the candlelight Susannah's face emerges near the window.

"Annie, bless you. Take the key back. Hurry. Then off to bed."

"But, miss, what will you –"

Susannah glides forward and leans close to the girl's frightened face. "The less you know the better," she hisses. "But thank you for this. Go!"

The girl's candlelight floods the tiny hall and then is gone. In the moonlight I see Susannah grab a small bag off the dresser and hurry to the open door, but then she stops – and I know she is looking toward me. I push the cover aside and follow.

Her shimmering figure descends the stairs, floats quickly down the hall and the second staircase, and out the back door. She doesn't run across the lawn, but moves furtively along the deep shadows at the edge of the yard. When she comes to the fountain and the pond, she disappears behind the dancing spray and reappears on the other side and then disappears again behind a lilac bush. She must be sitting on the stone seat. I circle the pond. There she is! I can see the glow of her white blouse. The gentle breeze shushes and drifts over the surface of the pond.

Together we wait. Are we too early? Are we too late?

There's a stealthy movement in the shadows.

"Nikos?" we whisper.

Her long white hand flutters to her throat.

"Yes, you should be surprised!" says a deep voice.

She stands up and cries, "Where is Nikos?"

"He's gone." Jeremy Fitzgerald steps into the moonlit clearing.

Susannah shakes her head. "No. He hasn't gone anywhere. He wouldn't —"

Jeremy Fitzgerald laughs. "Oh, he's gone all right. We warned you, Susannah. Your father and I have your best interests at heart. You are to be *my* wife. The wedding date is settled ..."

It's the same scene I saw two days ago. I know what he's going to say next. I know her words before they leave her mouth.

"No! He wouldn't! You're lying! Like Papa. You're

both liars!"

He leans over her. "He couldn't wait to get away …"

I press my hands over my ears and squeeze my eyes shut, but I can still hear Susannah's cry. "No. No! NO!" When I open my eyes again I'm sure they'll be gone, but they aren't. Susannah tries to run past him, but he catches her by the wrists.

"Let me go!" Her voice is terrified. "I have to find him! Let me go!"

"He's gone. He left you."

She twists out of his grip, but he blocks her and grabs one arm. Sobbing loudly, she pulls and pulls, but she isn't strong enough. I want to help her, but I can't move. "Susannah!" My words are sucked away into the night air.

As they struggle, he keeps repeating, "You aren't going with him! You aren't going with him, do you hear me? Do—you—hear—me?"

With each word he pushes her back until she is forced to step up onto the limestone slabs around the pond. Their feet slide on the wet stones, putting them both off balance. Like a slow-motion film, they fall into the water, Susannah dropping backwards under his weight. Her head strikes one of the stones. The terrible thud echoes through the night air. Then they both disappear under the water.

Jeremy Fitzgerald surfaces first and, waist deep, searches for her, frantically splashing his arms through the water and shouting her name. When he stops suddenly and reaches down to his shoulders, I know he's found her.

He drags her limp body back across the stones, sobbing,

"I told you! You should have listened to me. You're not going with him." He crouches over her, shaking her. "You're not going with him! Do you hear me? Do you hear me, Susannah?"

Susannah's head wobbles on her slender neck, her wet hair streaming blood.

"Susannah!" I scream.

Jeremy tries to make her stand, but she falls back in his arms like a rag doll. He cries her name and carries her to the stone seat and presses his shaking fingers to the side of her neck. Then he stands and slowly backs away, wiping his hands over and over on the front of his soaking jacket.

"You should have listened to your father and me. You should have listened," he keeps repeating in a thick choked voice.

"What have you done!" a voice bellows from behind me. Nikos rushes past Jeremy. He gently lifts Susannah and examines her head, before he, too, presses a shaking hand to her neck. For a moment he remains perfectly still, then with a roar he throws himself at the other man.

Fitzgerald swings wildly and catches Nikos on the side of the head, knocking him to his knees. Nikos shakes his head like an injured animal.

"If you come near me again," Fitzgerald says, viciously, "I'll tell them you killed Susannah. I'll tell them you murdered her out of jealousy. I'll tell them you've attacked her before. The old man will back me up!"

Nikos lurches to his feet. He stares at Fitzgerald,

uncomprehendingly. "You did this. You!"

"But I'll tell them it was you – and they'll believe me. If you run it will be proof of your guilt. They'll find you. They'll hang you." Spittle runs down Fitzgerald's chin.

"You did this to my Susannah," Nikos repeats. "You!"

Jeremy's back straightens and his voice is firm, but hysteria still burns at the edge of each word. "You're going to help me *now*. You have to. We'll bury her and –"

"No!" Nikos's bellow bursts inside my head.

"No!" There is a creaking tearing sound and something dark slams into me. I am nothing.

Chapter Thirty-eight

When I wake up I am standing on shaky legs not far from the old garden shed. How did I get here? Close by are the dull thumps of stone hitting stone.

Near the shed are two men. One piles stones onto a low mound of rocks and soil, while the other shovels loose dirt and gravel over it.

Nikos throws the shovel across the mound. It clatters at Jeremy Fitzgerald's feet.

"You go now. I want to be here with her." His voice is low-pitched and cold.

"I'm not taking my eyes off you."

"What we are doing is very wrong. She will never forgive us."

"She's dead, you stupid fool. She can't do anything to us. And she can't go away now, can she?" Jeremy starts to giggle. "And *you* won't hang for something I did!" His laughter rises and twists into the air like a snake.

Nikos stares at him, his eyes receding darkly into their sockets. Then, as if a faint light has been cast upon his grief, the features change and in a clear strong voice he says, "I don't care what happens to me. This is wrong. I will take whatever comes. She cannot be left here."

He scrabbles around in the stones, throwing them aside. They slam into each other with hollow clunks.

"Be quiet, you fool!" Jeremy hisses. "Stop it!"

"We must go to the police. We must take her to her father. I will make it right."

I stare with wide-prickling eyes as Fitzgerald picks up the shovel.

"I'll make it right!" He leaps over the stones, the shovel above his head.

I scream, "Look out!"

The shovel's handle strikes Nikos on the shoulder and slams him to his knees. Pain floods his face with horrified surprise. He rolls onto his back and the second blow just misses him and crashes the metal blade of the shovel onto the rocks beside his head. Fitzgerald lifts the shovel again, but as it swishes through the air, Nikos's hand grabs it. His other hand follows, and with a mighty heave, he wrenches it from Fitzgerald's grip and drags it through the air. With a sickening thud it strikes the other man's head. Fitzgerald crumples to the ground.

The sounds of rocks and earth and metal on stone, the smell of freshly turned soil, all fuse in my mind, and I feel as if I'm going to explode. I stumble toward the house. Halfway across the lawn, I stop.

No. I have to finish this, once and for all. I retrace my steps. The stone mound that was Susannah's secret grave is gone, the fountain has stopped, and the pond water is quiet and clogged with weeds.

I'm too late.

CHAPTER THIRTY-NINE

Maybe Lucas is back. Surely this couldn't have happened without him, could it? In less than a minute I'm in front of the cottage.

"Lucas? Are you home?" My voice is squeaky and thin.

A flutter of movement to one side of me, and my heart stops. A man moves slowly down the path toward the river and the trees. He is carrying another man over his shoulder like an enormous doll, the arms swinging loosely, the head banging against his back.

On shaky legs, I follow – staying in the darkest shadows. When I near the spot where Nikos made the cut with his shovel I hear the sounds of digging and I step behind a tree to watch.

Lucas is in the clearing, shovel in hand, staring at the man with the body of his enemy over his shoulder.

He sees me, but his eyes flick back to the man.

"Why didn't you tell me the truth?" he demands.

Nikos places the body of Jeremy Fitzgerald at Lucas's feet. Nikos? It can't be!

"I had lost her. It didn't matter." His voice is slow and

slightly garbled, as if he hasn't spoken for a long time.

"You killed Fitzgerald," Lucas says accusingly. "And then you took his name, his identity, everything he owned, didn't you? You went where no one knew you. And you married and had a son and you gave him — my father — the name Fitzgerald. And my father gave *me* the name Fitzgerald."

"He killed her. He was a terrible man. He overheard Susannah and me earlier that night. He came to me when I was packing. He knocked me unconscious and locked me in the cottage. She was waiting for me, and I couldn't be there when she needed me! When I came to, I smashed a window and crawled through. But I was too late. She was dead." Nikos covers his face with his hands and great sobs resound through the small space.

"But you killed him, Grandpa!"

Nikos straightens, arms at his side. "He would have killed me."

"And you buried him here," Lucas says, touching the soil with the tip of his shovel.

His grandfather, Nikos, nods. "Yes. It is not me who dies. I keep on living, even when I don't want to. I become Jeremy Fitzgerald. I work on my accent. I tell people that I had an Irish father and a Greek mother and that I grew up in Greece. They have no reason not to believe me. No one from his country comes to look for him. All sorts of people come to Canada and never return or write home. I know I am safe. I cut my hair and lose weight. I take a wife who bears a son and who leaves me because I cannot love her. Every day of my life I weep for what I have done and cannot undo. For what might have been. For my Susie. She couldn't save herself. I couldn't save her. I was too weak."

"She's been looking for you," Lucas says.

"No. It can't be so. I left her. All my life I have been waiting to see her again. To beg her forgiveness, knowing I don't deserve it. I ran away. I left her — alone. Lost. Because I am a coward! I've called outside her room, but no one comes. She will never forgive me."

In a low voice, Lucas asks, "What do you want me to do, Grandpa?"

"I have been through my actions again, hoping that somehow, by some miracle, I could get just one second to change things. But I can't. I can't change anything. Bring my body back here. Put me near her. I know I can't ask for more."

Lucas drops the shovel and steps toward his grandfather. "Grandpa …"

The heavyset man dissolves and in his place stands a thin man with short cropped white hair and large dark eyes.

I hear my voice say, "Follow me. Please — follow me. I'll take you to her."

He looks at me, his thin face filled with hope. I turn and walk toward Susannah's garden, to the pond where she waited with such happiness and trust.

Disappointment makes my chest so tight I can't breathe. She isn't here. There is no one here. "Susannah?" I call, but no one answers.

"I'm sorry," I say to the dim figure of the old man and to Lucas standing behind him. Lucas holds my hand tightly in his. "I thought ..."

But Nikos is gazing toward the stone seat. Suddenly, profound surprise and radiance travel over his features, and he becomes the young Nikos again — strong and alive.

"Susannah. Susie."

He walks past me, and when I turn to look he is gone. A great ache rises in my throat. "Did it work?" I whisper. "Did it?"

A voice, light and happy, whispers in my ear, "Yes. Yes, it did. Thank you, Thea, thank you."

As I turn to look at Lucas the voice drifts away into the silvery air. "Remember me ..."

Epilogue

"Look!" I say fiercely to Lucas. "These stupid chrysanthemums weren't here four days ago, or those pink day lilies. I wish they'd *tell* me when they're going to move something. No one's supposed to transplant flowering plants in *August*. How do they get away with it? I wanted to put dahlias in this spot come spring."

I throw down my trowel and shout into the air around us. "I don't mind a few things being moved! But, jeez, let me do something without you guys fiddling with it. Let me do it *my* way sometimes. If something doesn't grow I'll figure out what's wrong myself. Okay? OKAY?"

No one answers. Lucas keeps digging at the grass edging, where we planned to widen the south perennial bed, one of the few places that gets sun all day. Why bother? No doubt our ghostly gardeners will put the clods of grass and dirt right back when we're asleep.

I jump when Ellie speaks up right behind me. "*Now* who're you yelling at?"

"Nobody," I growl. "What do you want? Can't you just do one little job? You don't need to keep running over here every two seconds."

"I don't wanna pick dead flower heads. It's no fun," she whines. "It's my garden too, you know. I should be able to do whatever I want. Like you."

I laugh. "Like me? I wish I *could* do whatever I wanted."

Her frown deepens. "I hate it when you talk about stuff I don't understand."

I pull a thistle from next to a lush stand of Shasta daisies. "I don't understand it either."

She whines louder. "See? You're doing it again."

"Just go pick the stupid dead heads."

Ellie narrows her eyes, her lips down-turned. "But we wanna be near you guys." She looks at Lucas and a delicate pink flushes her thin cheeks.

Wee has crept up beside her, knees and fingers covered in dirt. She's in good whiney form, too. "You come see what I do, Thea. Bunch of deady heads in big pail. You come be with Wee, okay? Not just stay with Lucas."

I sigh. Teaching her to speak in fuller sentences has had its drawbacks. "Listen, you two asked to help. I didn't ask *you*. If you don't want to do the job right then go inside. You're driving me nuts!"

Lucas looks over at me. "Hey, take it easy, Thea."

"Oh yeah, right. Mr. Nice Guy. You never get mad, do you? Not even at Susannah and Nikos. And they're worse than these two – *they* can't leave anything alone!"

"Who're Susannah and Nikos?" Ellie asks. "You two talk about them, but you always shut up when I come near –"

"Go away!" I shout. Both faces drop. Wee's mouth trembles. "Look, I'm sorry. It's just that —"

From behind me Lucas clears his throat. "I'll give you each a penny for every dead flower head you pick. Would that help? There must be hundreds there."

"Yea!" Wee cries, and runs back the way she came.

"She's going to beat you to it," Lucas says to Ellie. She looks at him with great sorrow before flouncing over to the shade of the apple tree where baby Selina's carriage stands. She peers nonchalantly at the baby through the bug screen and then casually walks toward the perennial bed, where she pushes Wee aside and begins to yank flower heads — dead *and* alive.

I sigh again. This late-August day has not been a good one. School starts again in less than a week. I thought Lucas would come with me, but Reverend Pikeskill and Doc have decided he isn't ready for all that noise and activity. Will he ever be ready?

The good part is that Lucas is staying here for the winter. The Whiteheads, a friendly pair of ancients, have agreed to let him stay in the cottage as long as he continues the gardening and helps with other odd jobs. After many discussions with Doc and the Whitcheads, Reverend Pikeskill has agreed to tutor Lucas and also help him with his high-school correspondence courses. Perfect for him. But what about me?

I try not to be impatient with him. After all, he puts up with me — but why can't he let me help him with *his* problem now? I know he's afraid to leave the garden. Sometimes I'm sure it's because Nikos and Susannah won't let him go.

With some of the money he inherited from Nikos he bought a double headstone for them — a soft pink marble with twined leaves on either side. Too bad they don't spend more time there. Maybe Lucas would be able to break free if they stayed away for a while.

My frustration toward them, which has been building over the past few weeks, bubbles up again. "Look at you, Lucas! Digging and working and sweating. What's the point? We mow the lawns and pull the weeds and buy the plants, but Susannah and Nikos get to do the fun stuff — planning and designing the garden. I haven't put in one lousy plant that *they* haven't moved!"

Lucas laughs. "We've only been reading up on plants over one summer. And face it, Susannah was the one who planted this garden."

I give up. He just doesn't get it. I sit down with a thump and leave the trowel where it lies. I'm not working any more today and that's final.

"Come on, Thea, don't be mad at them." Lucas looks down at me sadly. "They let you clear the entire front yard and put in the corner rock garden there. And they didn't bother you once."

"No, because they've decided it's my territory. *They* don't care about going out into the open front yard." Then I mutter, "Just like you."

His look of sadness deepens. "That's not fair, Thea."

"Well, it's true! You go from the cottage to the Whiteheads' yard to this yard. That's all. We have picnics and we play badminton and croquet, but you never want to *leave*."

I don't add that the one thing I do look forward to is our evenings in his little house or by the pond. He and Reverend Pikeskill got the fountain going and, well, it's pretty romantic in the moonlight. But once I start back at school – when I leave the garden – what will happen to *us?*

He sticks his pitchfork deep into the soft earth. "I feel safe here. I hardly ever hear voices or sounds anymore – except Grandpa and Susannah. They talk together all the time. He's blissful. Susannah's a bit restless at times, but the garden makes her very happy. It ... I don't know ... I guess it comforts me, too."

I don't remind him that Susannah has no choice, that she and Nikos have nowhere else to go. Besides, maybe they're doing what they were *meant* to do.

Doesn't Lucas have a choice? I don't want to spend every single day of my life in this garden – not anymore – but I do want to be with him. It's like he's growing roots in this black soil. It's like Reverend Pikeskill and Doc have given him an excuse to hide in this safe hidden space.

"Should I dig this even wider?" he asks.

I shrug. "Why ask me? If they don't like it, they'll just change it. This garden doesn't belong to us. It's theirs. We have to find our *own* place. At least *I* do."

A soft breeze lifts a few reddish leaves off the lawn. They circle my head and flutter past my face. I feel a soft nudge against my shoulder and hear a whisper — "Take him with you. Don't leave him behind."

The hair on the back of my neck shivers. I can't get used to it even after all this time. Susannah let me know she was pleased when I took down the paintings, only framing four and hanging them over new wallpaper in my room. Two of hers and two of mine — *The Garden: Before and After*. But she kept taking down the portraits of her and Nikos. "Your room," she whispered each time. So, instead, I hung the portraits of Ellie and Wee and Lucas that I did over the summer.

Another nudge from behind. "Okay, okay," I mutter.

"What?" Lucas frowns at me.

"Let's go for a walk — just to the corner. Get an ice-cream from the Bridge Shop. Agatha can look after the kids. We deserve a break, right?"

He doesn't look at me. "I'd like to get this done before —"

"Before what? The snow falls?"

He rests one hand on the garden fork. "I ... I can't."

"Lucas ... soon I'll be leaving every day, and then winter will come. What will you do? Just sit in the cottage?"

"I'll have my schoolwork. And I'll have the driveway and sidewalks to shovel. And —"

"But I'll be gone every day! And at night there may be other things to do — movies, plays ... dances."

"I *can't,* Thea. It's better here. I feel safe with Nikos and Susannah."

"They don't want you here all the time!" I snap.

"How do you know?" Under the tan, his face turns pale.

"Sit down. You're giving me a crick in the neck."

Reluctantly he kneels beside me. The girls are shouting at each other about what flower heads belong in whose pile. At the same time, the carriage rocks back and forth and a tiny wail rises out of it. They've woken up Silly. Yes, poor little Selina with the pointed chin and shock of coal-black hair. My new little sister – Silly. Poor kid.

"If the voices start again, if they crowd in on me again," Lucas begins, "I may lose control. Doc says it won't happen, but I'm afraid ... of going away in my head and not being able to ... *be* with you. Doc says I have to try to go away from the garden a little at a time –"

"He did?" I can't believe my ears.

"He wants me to start to live a ... normal life, but I don't think I can, Thea."

"You told me once that you watched me for two weeks before my accident."

"Yeah, I did."

"And you said sometimes I'd hide behind a hedge and stare out across the river as if the whole world was out there and I'd never get to see it. Remember?"

He looks at me warily.

"Well, that's what's happening to you," I say. "I see you looking at the girls coming home from the swimming pool or at my parents rushing in and out of the driveway. I can tell you wish you could go somewhere, too — see what's out there. I could help you."

"I don't know …"

I stand up. "You also said in that poem, *The Lady of Shalott*, that it's love that takes the lady out of the shadows into the real world. Couldn't happen in real life, right?"

"Love has nothing to do with this," he says, his voice flat. He's moving into his private world.

"Fine!" I shout. "Forget it!"

The girls stop their squabbling and stare at me as if I've suddenly turned into the rusty wheelbarrow. Only Silly's wail continues, a little louder now.

Lucas's distant look changes into alarm. "Thea, hey — come on!"

"No. *You* come on — with me. I'm going out of this garden and down the street. For half an hour, that's all. Are you coming or not? I don't want to be that girl on the riverbank anymore. I'm not going to miss out on life, Lucas."

He looks up at me, his eyes afraid. "What if I —"

"I'll be there. I'll watch out for you. I won't let anything happen to you. I *won't*."

He eases to his feet. "Just half an hour?"

"Yes. One half hour. That's all — every day."

Before he can answer, a voice calls from the house. "Thea!"

I grit my teeth. Agatha's standing at the back door, a sweater over her shoulders.

"What do you want?"

"I've had a pretty intense session," she calls. "I thought I'd meet a friend for coffee, okay? Would you keep an eye on the girls? Silly's crying. She probably needs a clean diaper. I'll be back in time to feed her."

She turns back into the house, but stops dead when I shout, "NO!"

"I beg your pardon?"

"No, I can't look after them. Lucas and I are going out."

She can't push this and she knows it. I've looked after the kids all day. The new nanny doesn't start until next week.

"Please, please, can't we come too?" Ellie begs, running toward me.

I shake my head firmly. "Not this time. Lucas and I want some time alone. How about if we bring you back ... two Popsicles each for all the work you've done."

"Yees!" squeals Wee.

Ellie stares at us with jealous eyes. "I don't want anything."

"Fine," I say, and turn to Lucas. "Ready?"

We walk around to the front of the house. Lucas takes my hand and grips it tightly. As we reach the front sidewalk a breeze nudges my shoulder, then I hear two voices at once — a faint ghostly one that whispers "Finally. At last ..." and another louder one that whines, "Okay, okay, you guys. I'll have one grape and one lime. And don't let them melt. I'm not doing this work for *nothing!*"